T0209271

the Baker's Tale

the Baker's Tale

Ruby Spriggs and the Legacy of Charles Dickens

THOMAS HAUSER

COUNTERPOINT | BERKELEY, CALIFORNIA

This is a work of fiction. Despite the incidental use of actual historical
figures and places, the characters and incidents portrayed
in this book are wholly fictional.

LIBRARY OF CONGRESS CATALOGING-IN-PUBLICATION DATA
Hauser, Thomas.
The Bakers Tale : Ruby Spriggs and the Legacy of Charles Dickens /
Thomas Hauser.
pages ; cm
ISBN 978-1-61902-598-1 (hardcover)
1. Bakers—England—London—Fiction. 2. London (England)—Social
conditions—19th century—Fiction. 3. London (England)—Social life and
customs—19th century—Fiction. I. Title.
PS3558.A759B35 2015
813'.54—dc23
2015009414

Paperback ISBN: 978-1-61902-829-6

Cover design by Faceout
Interior design by Neuwirth & Associates

Counterpoint Press
2560 Ninth Street, Suite 318
Berkeley, CA 94710
www.counterpointpress.com

For Ruby Carellie Chapman
and
Reece Edwin Chapman

AUTHOR'S NOTE

This is a work of fiction. Throughout the manuscript, I have comingled the words of Charles Dickens with my own. I have also drawn from the May 1842 report of the Royal Commission headed by Lord Anthony Ashley that investigated the conditions in England's mines.

Thomas Hauser
New York, NY
2015

In the winter of 1836, I held an infant in my arms. The child, a girl eight months of age, was living under the most deplorable conditions that existed in London at that time. Since then, I have often wondered what happened to the child.

CHARLES DICKENS

Written at sea while returning home to England from America
April 1868

the Baker's Tale

Book 1

CHAPTER 1

The night passed. The stars grew pale. The day broke, and the winter sun rose over London on a cold day in January in the year of our Lord eighteen hundred and thirty-nine.

A white frost lay upon the ground. The sun looked down upon the ice that it was too weak to melt and hid behind a veil of clouds. Trees shuddered as blasts of wind howled and shook their bare branches. It was harsh, sharp, piercing, bitter, cutting, biting, cold.

I am not a well educated man, but I am wiser than some people take me for. I have an interest in many things and have taught myself what I can. I am a plain man and a practical man. That is my way.

I am a baker by trade. My labour in the bakery starts in the dark hours of morning. I rise early and breakfast by candlelight. The bakery is in a fashionable part of London. Servants come early and wait for the first bread and rolls to come out of the oven.

Bread is the best of all foods and one of the oldest foods known to man. It is spoken of hundreds of times in the Bible, twenty-three times in the Book of Genesis alone. It is the first thing asked for in the Lord's Prayer taught by Jesus to his disciples.

In London, as in much of the world, there is a harrowing disparity between rich and poor. Wealth and poverty, repletion and starvation, exist side by side.

At times, the classes are intertwined. In the fourteenth century, the Black Death borne by rats killed one of every three people in London. Three hundred years later, again borne by rats, the Great Plague came. Thousands of corpses were carried in death carts and buried together in huge unmarked graves. In 1666, much of London was destroyed by the Great Fire, one of several times that flames have brought the city to its knees.

But among the poor, ignorance is a greater curse than plague or fire. There the divide between the classes looms large. The absence of learning and want of knowledge is a constant cause of misery among the downtrodden. Ignorance is the reason the poor live— that is to say, they have not yet died—in ruinous places on dangerous streets that are avoided by all but those who live there. On winter days when the sun shines, their hovels are colder than the outdoors.

Others among the poor are without shelter of any kind. They wander through long weary nights, counting the chimes of church clocks from hour to hour. They listen to the rain and crouch for warmth in doorways and beneath old bridges. They watch lights twinkling in chamber windows, thinking of the children coiled there in beds and the comfort that these children enjoy.

Their lives are unlightened by any ray of hope. Every aspiration blights and withers before it can grow. They were poor before. They are poor now. They will be old and poor before they know it. From birth to grave, their path is narrow.

Their life of poverty knows no change and no goal but that of struggling in toil for bread. A poor man labours to gain food for himself and for his family from day to day. His children cry with hunger. They plead for bread. Not the daily bread of the Lord's Prayer as prayed for in London's richest congregations where it is understood to include half the luxuries of the world. They plead for as much food as will support life, a crust of dry hard bread that is often just beyond their reach.

❦

The wind was blowing harder now. Men and the few women who were on the streets bent down their heads to defend against its stinging arrows. A light snow began to fall and joined with the frozen crust upon the ground.

Then I saw a man and child standing outside the bakery.

The man was attired in coarse rough clothes. His coat was of a size that had not been made for him and had come to such a state that it was impossible to know its original colour. It was ragged at the edges and seemed too thin to keep him warm. His eyes spoke of long hard endurance and dreadful hunger.

The child was a girl between the ages of three and four. Like the man, she was wearing common clothes. Her coat was patched with rag and her shoes with straw. A shawl had been wrapped around her shoulders and chest in an effort to keep her warm.

It was the child that captured my attention. Such hardness as I might summon up to sustain me against the miseries of adults fails when I look at children. I see how young and defenseless they are against the injustices of the world.

Several of the child's fingers pushed through holes in her mittens. The young endure these things better than the old. But like the man, the child was shivering. She clung tightly to his bare hand and kept close to him.

Man and child gazed with hungry eyes at the bread behind the window. Bread guarded by a sheet of glass that was a brick wall to them. Then the man came to the door.

As a rule of business, I do not give to beggars. But the strong affection between the man and child touched my emotions. I allowed him in.

"Begging your pardon, sir. Could I do labour for you in exchange for a loaf of bread?"

My answer was slow in coming.

"Please, sir. The child is hungry, and it is wrong that she should suffer. I will do anything for bread for the child."

There is a table in the rear of the bakery where I sometimes sit and engage in conversation. The apprentice boy was on duty in the front, which gave me the freedom to converse. Had it been otherwise, everything would have happened differently and I would not have this tale to tell.

I led the man and child past loaves of bread, rolls, pastries, and other goods of my trade. The smell of coffee and freshly baked bread filled the air.

There was a warm fireplace by the table in back. Sometimes we are hungry. Sometimes we are frightened. But cold is often hardest upon us.

The man sat by the fire and opened his hands to receive its warmth. The child took off her mittens and did the same.

He was of average height, well made with intelligent eyes and a muscular frame grown thin.

"What is your name?"

"Spriggs, sir. Christopher Spriggs."

"And the child?"

"Ruby."

"She is your daughter?"

"No, sir. My niece."

"And her parents?"

"She has none."

I extended my hand.

"My name is Antonio."

I put two mugs on the table. One with coffee from a pot above the fire, the other with milk for the child. Then I cut two thick slices of bread, one for Christopher, the other for Ruby.

His eyes met hers with a reassuring look.

Ruby took the bread, clenched it in her little hand, and ate as though nothing else in the world mattered. Not ravenously. She chewed and swallowed each bite. But after each swallow, she immediately took another bite.

When the bread was gone, she smiled.

There was a glow about her. Had she been wrapped in a blanket, it would have been impossible for the haughtiest stranger to differentiate between her and a child of the highest rank in society. As for her smile, a blessing from the Archbishop of Canterbury would have done no more to warm my heart.

"Where do you live?" I asked.

"In no place long," Christopher responded.

"And the child's parents?"

"Her mother, my sister, was a good woman. She died of fever a year ago. The father was there only on the night of conception."

"Are there only two of you?"

"Only two."

As we conversed, Ruby's eyes rested upon mine with an expression of wondering thoughtfulness that is seen sometimes in young children.

Christopher did not eat his bread. I know when a man is hungry. I can see it in his eyes.

"Eat. I will give you more for Ruby to take home."

The bread that I had given to him was quickly gone.

"I would like to work for what we have eaten," he said.

"Not today. But you have come at the right time. Perhaps it is fate. Be here tomorrow at ten o'clock in the morning. There may be a job and more for you."

I gave Christopher the rest of the loaf of bread to take home. He and Ruby left. I knew the world they were retreating to. The streets are mean and close. Poverty and misfortune fester. Hunger and want had surrounded Ruby Spriggs from the first dawning of her reason.

That night, she would not leave my thoughts. I was anxious for her return.

CHAPTER 2

I was born in London in 1801. King George III sat upon the throne. The French still owned a portion of America as vast as the original colonies. Lord Nelson's victory over the French and Spanish fleets was in the future. A practical steamship had yet to be built.

My father was a British seaman who married a beautiful Italian woman and brought her back to England. Unfortunately, I inherited my father's looks. When I was five years old, my mother fled England with an Italian nobleman. I never saw her again. If she had been the wife of a king, war would have followed. But since she was only my father's wife, the affairs of state went on uninterrupted.

The schools in England are for people of means, which I was not. It was expected that I would live my life as a labourer, unable to read or write. Then, in my eighteenth year, I met a man named Octavius Joy.

Mr. Joy made a great deal of money in honest finance. He was a brilliant man of scrupulous veracity with regard to numbers. Once he had earned his fortune, he set out to spend it.

"People are anxious to be employed and fairly paid for their labour," Mr. Joy said. "Those who work hard and are able to provide for their families through fairly paid labour are likely to be content. I have seen men whose lives were lived under the worst privation and suffering become happy and at peace when they were given work to do and were fairly compensated."

In keeping with this belief, Mr. Joy put common men and women in situations where they learned the skills necessary to run a business. When their skills were sufficient, he placed them in a business of their own. "I seek to leave them," he explained, "not with resources that can be easily spent but with skills that place them beyond the reach of poverty forever."

It was also important to Mr. Joy that people learn to read and write. He expressed this view with the declaration, "Reading is a passageway to knowledge. All men and women should be able to read, write, and perform simple arithmetic. They should be able to keep accounts. That is, they should be able to put down in words and figures the cost of what they need to live and how much money they have to spend. I hope for a day when all children in England regardless of their class are taught to read and write. Reading and writing, knowledge of the world, the spread of ideas. That is the key to everything."

In keeping with this philosophy, Mr. Joy established a learning center in London. Common men and women and their children were welcome to attend free classes in reading that were taught six days a week from eight o'clock in the morning until eight o'clock at night.

I was a labourer in Covent Garden market when Mr. Joy took me off the streets. At his direction, I apprenticed in a bakery. I learned the trade and, at his insistence, I also learned to read and write. Then Mr. Joy placed me in a bakery of my own.

"You are to follow four principles in the operation of your business," he instructed. "One: good quality food is to be prepared and sold. Two: each person you employ is to be fairly paid. Three: all bills for purchases by the bakery are to be paid weekly. Four: every person who walks through the bakery door is to be treated with dignity and respect."

Remarkably, Mr. Joy refused any profit from the businesses that he helped establish.

"I am rich," he said. "I take no pleasure in hoarding and have more than enough to ensure comfort for the rest of my life. I would be ashamed to touch what has been earned through the hard labour of another man."

"What is your motive in this?" he was once asked.

"Always fishing for motives when they are right on the surface," Mr. Joy responded. "The motive is plain. To make people useful and happy. It brings me great pleasure to see people who are achieving the most that they can out of their natural abilities. I do not believe in the Bible as the absolute word of God, and I am particularly suspicious of those who seek to impose their own interpretation of the Bible upon us. But I do believe that we should do unto others as we would wish them to do unto us were we in their shoes."

Christopher and Ruby returned to the bakery at ten o'clock on the day after we met.

"Good morning, little one," I addressed the child. "You look fresher today than a spring flower."

She smiled. No view in England was as enticing.

I gave them bread, coffee, and milk, as I had done the day before.

At eleven o'clock, Octavius Joy arrived. He was a man of sixty, portly with a round, good-humoured, benevolent face that was full of life and radiated an almost innocent happiness that would have been delightful in a child and was particularly appealing in a man his age. His cheeks were rosy, a colour occasioned in part by the cold. His hair was a silvered grey. Looking at him, one might have forgotten for a moment that there was such a thing as a sour mind or a crabbed countenance in the world.

We sat at the table in back. Mr. Joy looked at Ruby through gold-rimmed spectacles and patted her on the head.

"What is your name, my dear?"

"Ruby."

"A very pretty name." Then he turned in my direction. "Perhaps Ruby would like another piece of bread and some strawberry jam."

I excused myself from the table and returned with the offering. Ruby's eyes took on a questioning look.

"When one is starving, jam is a luxury beyond reach," Christopher said. "She has never seen jam before."

"Eat," he told Ruby. "You will like it."

Ruby cautiously took a bite . . . Tasted the jam on her tongue . . . And her face lit up.

This was a child who, for her entire life, had eaten only to survive. Mother's milk in her first year. Then bread, gruel, and an occasional potato, green leaf, or piece of cheese. Now, for the first time, she was experiencing food as pleasure rather than just for sustenance.

"Good!" she cried out. "Good! Good!"

Octavius Joy laughed. Then he turned to Christopher.

"Antonio visited me last night and told me of your circumstances. Tell me your history in your own words."

There was something so earnest in the way this was said and with such disregard of the class differences between them that Christopher felt at ease. He spoke. Mr. Joy listened attentively and, when the narrative was done, put his hand on Christopher's shoulder.

"Let me make an offer to you, something that may change your life for the better. I have made it my concern to place men and women who come from hard origins in situations where they can live decently as a consequence of their own honest labour. One of the people I assisted in this manner is a woman named Marie Wells. Marie and her husband were the proprietors of a bakery in a nearby part of London. Mr. Wells died suddenly four weeks ago. Marie is a good woman and in need of help. There is a job for you at the bakery. You and Ruby would live there. You would have food to eat, a small salary, and a home."

Christopher seemed at a loss for words.

"I would like that very much," he said at last.

"And there is another condition of your employment. You and Ruby must learn to read."

"It is my dream that Ruby learn to read and write. But for me, it is beyond my comprehension."

"At the moment, it is also beyond Ruby's comprehension. That will change for both of you. Reading will come more easily to her because she is young and will be without the fear that you bring to the adventure. But what a child can learn, you can learn too."

"And if I cannot?"

"When the opportunity presents itself, learning to read is a responsibility that you have to yourself. Learning to read is like entering a dark room and lighting a candle. It will light the fire of your imagination. You need not learn to read well, only as well as honest effort on your part allows."

"I will try."

"Then it is settled. Marie must first approve of you, but I think she will. She needs a man's help in the bakery, and she has long wanted a child in her life. I spoke with her this morning. She is expecting our visit now."

The most common form of public transportation in London is the omnibus. The public gets on and off as the vehicle is drawn along its route by horses. Hackney coach stands offer licensed public cabs for those who prefer their own coach and driver.

Mr. Joy summoned a hackney coach. Christopher, Ruby, and I joined him inside.

"We are going to meet a very nice woman named Marie," Mr. Joy told Ruby. "Last night, Antonio told Marie that you are very nice, and she would like to meet you."

The cold of the previous day had lifted a bit. Mr. Joy and Ruby got along exceedingly well as the carriage clattered through the streets of London. Of course, Mr. Joy got along exceedingly well with everyone. Fifteen minutes after our ride began, we arrived at Marie's bakery.

I have known Marie for many years. She is two years younger than I am and one of the kindest people I know. Anyone who casts even a casual glance upon her can discern that she has a loving heart. Her serene blue eyes and gentle face bespeak her nature. She has the good opinion and respect of all who know her.

Mr. Joy introduced Christopher to Marie, and she explained the operation of the bakery to him in simple terms. Then she and Ruby played together.

"You and the child are to be here tomorrow morning with all of your belongings," Mr. Joy told Christopher at day's end.

Marie added a promise to that instruction.

"If you live in my home, Ruby will have the best of care and the most love that I can give her."

The following morning, Christopher and Ruby arrived at Marie's bakery with a small cloth bag. The whole of their worldly belongings—the discarded clothes of others and a tiny doll not much more than a rag—were inside.

Octavius Joy had given money to Marie to buy Ruby some better clothes. Christopher would wear the clothes that had belonged to Marie's husband.

"It would make you sad to see me in them," Christopher protested.

"It would give me pleasure to know that they are well used."

Marie led Christopher and Ruby to the floor above the bakery and showed them the living quarters. There were two rooms, each with a simple wood bed that consisted of a platform and mattress filled with straw. Like the beds, the other furniture was of little worth but sufficient and neatly kept. Christopher and Ruby would sleep in one room. Marie would sleep in the other.

Ruby had never seen a bed before.

Marie washed Ruby's face, combed her hair, and made the rest of her as fresh and clean as a child can be. At day's end, she prepared dinner.

There is a soft place in my heart for Marie. She is like family to me. I had been invited to share this occasion with her and her new family.

The fire burned clear. The kettle boiled. The table was set.

Ruby did not know what it was like to sit down for a meal at an appointed hour. In the past, she had eaten whenever there was food.

"This is where we eat our meals," Marie explained.

"Every day?"

"Every day."

If a child of three can be said to contemplate, Ruby contemplated the meaning of those words.

After dinner, Christopher moved his chair closer to the fire and sat with a look of contentment on his face. The room was warm. One of the logs broke in two and blazed up as it fell. Another log was thrown on.

"I am grateful beyond anything that I can express," Christopher said as he pondered the change that had come upon his life. "If ever I can prove to you the truth of those words, I will."

Seen with the fire behind her, Ruby looked as though she had a glory shining round her head.

Then it was time for her to sleep. One night earlier, Ruby had shivered in the cold on rags placed on a hard dirt floor. Now she would slumber in the warmth of her bed, as humble as it was.

Marie lay Ruby down on the bed and wrapped a blanket round her. Warmth, shelter, and peace were there.

Then a look that I am unable to describe stole across Ruby's face.

"Ruby and uncle stay," she said.

The words were spoken as both a question and a plea.

"Ruby and uncle stay," she said again with anxiety rising in her voice.

"Ruby and uncle stay," Marie pledged.

Ruby smiled a smile of relief.

There are moments of unmixed happiness in our lives that cheer our transitory existence on earth. This was one of them.

Marie had the child that she had longed for but thought would never come. And Ruby Spriggs had a home.

I made a silent promise to myself that, whatever happened in my life, I would help care for this child.

"Good night, little one," I said. "Pleasant slumber. Happy dreams. May angels guard your bed."

Ruby fell asleep with a smile on her face. I fancied that she was dreaming.

CHAPTER 3

Christopher had sought honest labour. Once it was found, he adapted well to the demands of a baker's life.

He learned first to mix yeast and water with grain—wheat, rye, barley—and to bake the dough for bread in the large brick oven. Before long, he was able to make rolls, muffins, and pastries. He had a way with people and engaged naturally in conversation with customers without lingering too long.

When I was a child, my father taught me to be industrious. I appreciate that quality in others. It is, in my opinion, one of the most charming qualities of the human character. Christopher applied himself to his new job with industriousness and effort. He was always active. When not otherwise engaged, he was cleaning. The tile floor and table in back and chairs and walls and oven were as clean as scrubbing could make them. Twice a day, he took a broom and swept up crumbs until there was not a speck on the floor. He showed intelligence by asking how things worked and fixing them when they were broken.

With his mind at ease and with adequate food, Christopher passed into a new state of being. His body filled out. The colour that had forsaken his face returned. Sometimes a look came into his eyes as though he were remembering the hardships of his past. He wrestled at times with the understanding that he could not give bread to every beggar who came to the door. But he seemed at peace with himself.

"I have never seen a man more hard working than he," Marie told me. "He does each thing until it is done right."

Reading came slowly. Christopher went to the learning center in the early evening twice each week. Marie and I did the best we could to help with his lessons. There was a wish on our part to teach and a desire on his part to learn. But at age twenty-seven, he found the road difficult to follow.

Often at night, he would stare at the symbols on a piece of paper that had been given to him:

A B C D E F G H I J K L M N O P Q R S T U V W X Y Z
a b c d e f g h i j k l m n o p q r s t u v w x y z

The alphabet is the building block for the English language. Christopher struggled with it as though each letter were a bramble-bush that scratched until it drew blood. He could not see the forest through the trees. When he tried to read, his bewildered eyes fixed on each letter rather than connecting the letters to syllables and the syllables to words and the words to sentences.

"It is hard to learn at this time of my life," he said.

"If you learned to talk, you can learn to read," Octavius Joy assured him. "I know you are struggling, but you must keep at it. If you entertain the notion that any great success was, or ever will be, achieved without effort, leave that wrong idea behind. Perseverance will gain the summit of any hill."

It is hard for people without hope to learn. They cannot see accomplishments and success in their future. But Christopher's new life had given him hope, and he soldiered on. When studying a lesson, he would take up a piece of chalk as though it were a large tool and roll up his sleeves as though wielding a crowbar or hammer. Then he would square his elbows, put his face close to his copy slate, and labour.

"Well, Christopher," I said on one occasion while looking over several copies of the letter "O," which he had represented as a square, a rectangle, and a triangle. "You are improving. If only you can get it to be round, it will be perfect."

A man must make the most of every opportunity he has in life. In time, Christopher began to read and write on a small scale. Letters became words. Words became sentences. Sentences fit into the context of passages that were understandable to him. From time to time, I saw him glance at the front page of a journal or the cover of a book with a curiosity that went beneath the binding.

He also showed a modest aptitude for fractions and decimals, which enabled him to weigh each loaf of bread in the presence of the buyer. Taken together, his newly acquired skills allowed him to master the sign on the bakery wall:

Slice of Bread or Roll	One Half-Penny
Bread or Roll and Butter	One Penny
Bread or Roll and Cheese	One Penny
Boiled Egg	One Penny
Muffins and Pastries	Price Varies
Cup of Tea or Coffee	One Penny

ALL ARTICLES OF THE BEST QUALITY

There are many kinds of pride. Christopher took pride in his labour. He took pride as he learned to read and write. But the greatest pride and joy in his life was Ruby.

Night after night, he sat with her. No matter how tired he was after a long day's work, he would take her on his back and carry her round in play. When he spoke to her, his voice was never rough or angry. His hands were large but never heavy when he touched her. Her smile always brightened his face, as if, when she smiled, they were coining gold.

A man of noble lineage loves the mansion of his inheritance as a trophy of birth and wealth. The root of a poor man's attachment to his home grows deep into purer soil.

Christopher saw his new home as a grandly furnished palace. And Ruby was as much at home as if she had lived there for her entire life. She knew nothing in a philosophical way about the inequities of society. But she knew that the world she had once lived in was a very hard place and her new world was very unlike it. Soon, all trace of the deprivation of her early years was gone.

Marie had lost the love of a husband but now had the love of a child. To see her walk hand in hand with Ruby, to watch them together in the home, warmed the heart. She would sing to Ruby when putting her to sleep. Ruby would smile and close her eyes. At times, I wondered if the child's mind might not be journeying back to the earliest years of her life when she was sung to by another woman who held her in her arms and called her "my child."

If a good fairy had built a home for Ruby with the wave of a magic wand and made her a princess in the bargain, she would not have been happier. Each day began with three eggs on the table. One for Ruby, one for Marie, and one for Christopher. There was bread, milk, and coffee. On Sundays, bacon or sausage hissed in a pan.

Children move back and forth between being free spirits totally immersed in a doll, a flower, or whatever has captured their fancy in the moment and, when sad, the most heavily burdened souls on earth. But the world was full of happiness for Ruby. She took joy in every tree, in every bird, in the sun by day and the stars at night. Her childish eyes opened wider and wider as she discovered more of the world round her. She was inquisitive and playful. She loved the church bells when they rang.

Unlike Marie, I lived alone. I have had some ladies on my arm and kissed more than a few in my time. But I never married. Marie and her husband were my family. Now Christopher became my brother and Ruby my child. I was invited often to join them for dinner. Marie made an honest stout soup with potatoes, rice, and barley. There was bread, cheese, greens when in season, and, once a week, meat.

Ruby frequently visited my bakery. On these occasions, the words "Ruby help," spoken by her with enthusiasm, inspired both a smile and dread. Invariably, she was soon up to her elbows in flour with more flour in her hair.

"Young lady," I told her. "You are not easy, but you are worth the trouble."

On one of her visits, I asked if she would like to help make strawberry jam. Not just eat it, but make it from scratch. A cry of joy escaped her lips, and two bright eyes fixed upon me in expectation.

We washed the strawberries, crushed them, and mixed them with sugar. Then I poured the mixture into a pan and stirred it over a flame until the sugar had fully dissolved.

The jam boiled for five minutes. As it was cooling, Ruby reached for the pan.

"Young lady; if you place a matter in the hands of a professional, you must not interfere with the conduct of his business.

The pan is hot. Leave it alone, do not burn yourself, and we will get along exceedingly well. But if you try again to touch it, I am going to eat you up like a big piece of bread with jam."

"I'm not bread with jam."

"No?"

"No! I'm a girl. I'm Ruby."

After the jam cooled, I spooned most of it into jars, sealed them with wax, and put the rest on bread for Ruby.

Here, I might add that jam has many uses.

"Ruby, we are going to clean the room together," Marie said one day.

"No!"

Marie's suggestion was repeated more strongly, this time as a command.

Ruby's "no" was repeated with equal conviction.

"No jam for you today," Marie warned.

"I do it! I do it!"

With Ruby under the same roof as Christopher and Marie, the smile of Heaven shone on the chamber. With her golden hair and sparkling blue eyes, she was like a beautiful springtime morning. Drops of rain that fell on her hair looked like dew freshly gathered on a flower. Smiles played upon her face like light upon jewels. She was affectionate and sweet-natured with a musical little voice. I do not know how she came to be that way. I can only say that she was blessed and that, in her earliest years, she must have been very much loved by her mother.

I loved that little girl so much. She could have been the daughter of a king.

We celebrated Ruby's fourth birthday in July. Christopher was crying that evening at dinner.

"She was the only thing that made this world of value for me," he said through tears. "And now, to see her so happy . . ."

Summer passed. Autumn leaves fell. Then came winter and Christmas.

Christmas encircles the small world of a child like a magic ring. This was a Christmas unlike any that Ruby and Christopher had known before.

Marie's bakery and my own opened for business on Christmas morning at the normal hour of seven o'clock. Three hours later, we closed our doors and I went to her home where gifts were exchanged.

Marie gave Ruby a pair of red mittens that she had knitted while Ruby was sleeping. Christopher gave her a doll. I brought a miniature rocking horse about the size of my hand. Then we left for a special occasion. Octavius Joy had invited us to his home for Christmas dinner.

The streets were sprinkled with clusters of people wearing their gayest faces and dressed in their finest clothes. I could only imagine how the sights and sounds echoed in Ruby's mind. The colours, the smiles, the good cheer.

We passed a group of carolers, singing in a language that Ruby did not understand:

> *Adeste Fideles laeti triumphantes,*
> *Venite, venite in Bethlehem.*

The voices were a beautiful orchestra to her.

"Christmas brings back the pleasures of our childhood," Marie said as she took my arm.

Mr. Joy lived in a large brick house in a fashionable part of London. A servant met us at the door and retreated to announce the arrival of Miss Ruby Spriggs. That was unnecessary, since Ruby had followed him inside and rushed to embrace Mr. Joy before the announcement.

"Thank you for coming," he told us. "Christmas is far more merry when viewed through the eyes of a child."

Everything in the house was beautifully kept. Holly and mistletoe were much in evidence. Mr. Joy led us into the parlour and introduced us to his other guests.

A large evergreen tree laden with ornaments rose to the ceiling. Rosy-cheeked dolls hid behind clusters of green needles. Jolly-faced little men perched among the boughs. Fiddles and drums dangled from branches. There was a star at the top.

Ruby stared in wonder.

Then it was time for gifts. I had asked for the honour of bringing rolls and pastries to accompany dinner. Ruby gave our host a portrait she had drawn, which Mr. Joy promptly declared was the finest likeness of himself that he had ever seen. Marie had knitted a scarf for him in Christmas colours. Christopher had fashioned a window box in which Mr. Joy's gardener could plant flowers in the spring.

Following that, it was Mr. Joy's turn to give. A music box for Marie. New coats for Christopher and myself. And for Ruby . . . A doll's house with an open front and three distinct rooms. A parlour, a bedroom, and kitchen. Each room had miniature furniture crafted from wood. The kitchen came with an assortment of diminutive utensils and a set of tiny platters with delicacies glued tight on top.

Ruby's eyes opened wide and her lower jaw dropped in the manner of a toy nutcracker. There was a cry of joy and the never-to-be-forgotten image of a wildly happy child.

Dinner was served. There were eighteen guests. Ruby was seated with Christopher and Marie on either side.

Mr. Joy spoke a brief blessing about Christmas being a time to remember the less fortunate and expressed the hope that someday part of the Christmas spirit would live in all hearts for all of the year.

During dinner, he engaged easily in conversation over a wide range of subjects from cheerful topics to more serious reflections. He adapted to whomever he was speaking with, whether that person was the wealthy banker seated to my left or Marie.

Mr. Joy also proved to be an expert at carving. A roast goose is universally acknowledged to be the greatest stumbling block to perfection in that science. Many aspiring carvers who began successfully with legs of mutton and enhanced their reputation through fillets of veal, quarters of lamb, and even ducks have been defeated by a roast goose.

To Mr. Joy, resolving a goose into its smallest component parts was a performing art. No handing the dish over to a servant, no hacking and sawing at an unruly joint. No noise, no splash. The legs of the bird slid gently down into a pool of gravy. The wings seemed to melt from the body. The breast separated into a row of juicy slices to reveal a cavern of stuffing.

When the meal was done, Mr. Joy turned to Ruby with a twinkle in his eyes.

"Come with me," he said. "I would not be surprised if we found a gingerbread soldier in the drawing room. Let us go and look for him."

It seemed to Ruby as if the drawing room was all nooks and corners. And in each nook and corner, there was some little chair or cupboard or something or other that made her think there could not possibly be such another good nook or corner in the room until she looked at the next one and found it equal to if not better than the one before.

Eventually, she found the gingerbread man and returned to the parlour with Mr. Joy. Port wine, plum pudding, cheeses, pastries, and roasted chestnuts were being served.

Then Ruby announced that she had a story to tell and recounted a tale that I believe was about a dragon, since I heard the phrase "bad dragon" several times and she snorted as though she were a dragon. At the close of the recitation, she shouted "bad dragon" one more time, exhaled as though dying, and with great drama lay down on the floor with her eyes closed and her arms across her chest.

There was applause, which she enjoyed immensely, after which she turned to Mr. Joy and announced that it was his turn to tell a story.

"Why don't I read you a story," he suggested.

Mr. Joy went to his study, returned with a book of fairy tales, put on his reading spectacles, and began.

"Once upon a time, there was a beautiful princess, who had everything she could wish for and a great deal more. The princess lived in a beautiful palace. She had gold and silver and diamonds—"

"And potatoes," Ruby interrupted.

"That's right. The princess had potatoes."

"And soup and bread and lots of jam."

"And what did the palace look like?" Mr. Joy inquired.

"The princess had her own bed," Ruby answered. "And there was a fireplace and everyone was happy."

As it should be in a fairy tale.

"What did the princess look like?" Ruby asked, summoning Mr. Joy to return to the narrative.

"Well," he told her, "she had eyes like Ruby and hair like Ruby and smiled like Ruby and laughed like Ruby."

"It was me," Ruby offered.

"And one day, Ruby left the palace on a magical journey."

"And then I met a dragon."

"That's right. Ruby met a dragon."

"A big dragon with fire in its mouth that jumped out of the woods. And I said to the dragon, 'Do you want to play with me?' And the dragon said yes, so I played with the dragon."

There was a pause.

"Read from the book," Ruby instructed.

"The sky was blue. The sun was bright. The water was sparkling. The leaves were green."

"And then I met another dragon," Ruby interrupted. "And this dragon didn't want to play with me. So the first dragon that was the nice dragon ate the bad dragon."

"I have seen many children in my life," Octavius Joy told us at day's end. "But never a child like Ruby."

Perhaps that is because there never was another child like Ruby. Of course, many people, I am sure, feel that way about their sons and daughters and other loved ones. So I will say simply that Ruby was an energetic, charming, exuberant, marvelous, ingratiating, indefatigable bundle of joy.

She took a child's delight in walking the streets and looking in shop windows. When a rare winter storm came to London, she and Christopher strolled about, leaving footprints in the freshly fallen snow on London Bridge above the River Thames. Her first shoes with laces were cause for celebration.

Like all children, she thought at times that she was the pivot on which the world turned. She drew a picture of my bakery that I affixed to the wall and, whenever she came to visit, gazed at the drawing with pride. She regarded each annual celebration of her birth as a well-earned distinction brought about as a consequence of her own monumental achievement.

She was unruly at times.

"Miss Spriggs," I chastised on one such occasion. "I am older than you and, some might think, wiser. Therefore, I will inform you that it is not the custom in London to put one's knife in one's mouth. The fork is reserved for that purpose, but is not to be inserted in the mouth further than necessary. Also, it is worthy of mention that, in polite society, the spoon is not used as a catapult to hurl small objects round the room."

And she could be stubborn. Most children in London were taught to read by their parents if they were taught at all. Marie helped Christopher with his lessons and began the process of teaching Ruby.

"I know the alphabet," Ruby told me. "A . . . B . . . C . . . D . . . Me."

"Now it is my turn," I said, seeking to gently correct her. "A . . . B . . . C . . . D . . . E—"

"No! A . . . B . . . C . . . D . . . Me."

"Ruby Spriggs, I regret to inform you that 'me' is not a letter in the English alphabet."

"Me."

"E."

"Me."

"Of all the obstinate, stubborn, wrong-headed little creatures that were ever born, you are the most so."

Stubborn, but gifted where letters were concerned.

The Church of England at that time held to the position that one should learn to read the Bible as part of the journey to salvation. To the extent that children were taught to read and write, it was most often through religious texts.

The learning center that Octavius Joy founded was a temple of good intentions with a different view. The center was open to men, women, and children of all ages with separate classes for children and adults. Reading was taught to the young with an eye toward Mother Goose and to adults through the reading of light classics and popular journals.

"I want those who come here to understand when they leave that reading is for pleasure as well as knowledge," Mr. Joy said.

Ruby learned the letters of the alphabet and the novelty of their shapes by sound and by sight. She had a gift for putting them together on paper, which she did with the deliberation of a bookkeeper and in a hand that was clear. She worked hard at her learning.

"A" is an archer. And also an apple. "B" is a ball. And also a boy. "C" is a cat. "D" is a dog." And so on through the zebra at the end of the alphabet.

Sometimes, the students at the learning center read aloud in chorus.

"The man has a hat . . . The man has a fat cat."

In time, that became "The . . . handsome . . . prince . . . held the . . . beautiful . . . princess . . . in his . . . arms . . . and . . . kissed her."

Often, Christopher sat beside Ruby at night and listened to her read until it was too dark for her to see the letters. And they would write sentences back and forth to one another on their slates.

"Ruby has a pretty dress . . . I love uncle."

Other times, Christopher read aloud to her, which he did as though the eyes of a significant portion of the population of London, if not all of England, were upon him.

And at times, he gave in to frustration.

"It is no use," he said one evening. "I try and I try. I think I can read, and then I cannot. What I read makes no sense. A cow cannot jump over the moon."

"And an old woman does not live in a shoe," Marie reminded him.

His face brightened. "Now I remember. It is a ha-ha."

And all the while, Ruby was growing older. The winds and tides rose and fell. The earth moved round the sun myriad times.

Ruby reached a certain age and moved her bed to share a room with Marie instead of Christopher.

Her blue eyes seemed bluer and her spirit even lighter than before. A prettier face, a more loving heart, never bounded so lightly over the earth. There was such joy in her laugh that the sternest misanthrope would have smiled in her presence. One could not fail to become attached to her. Her charm and grace were enough to make a prison cheerful.

She wore plain clothes, but had the carriage of a princess when she wore them. Young children clustered at her skirts. Old men and women spoke a friendly greeting when she passed. She remained devoted in attachment to Marie and Christopher. And the crowning glory of it all was that she was without guile and seemed totally unaware of how delightful she was.

When Ruby was young, little boys had fallen in love with her, often making gifts of small trinkets, nuts, and apples. Now came attention of a similar kind from boys who were older. She kissed a few but nothing more.

"You have your mother's look of beauty," Christopher told her. "You are to tell me, not only if you ever fall into trouble, but also when you fall in love."

He and I met on occasion for a glass of ale. Once, as we drank, he spoke to me of Ruby's mother.

"She was a beautiful woman, whose life was destroyed by a madman. It is all in the police records. It is not necessary for Ruby to know."

He continued to work cheerfully in the bakery from sunrise until dark. As Ruby grew older, she often worked with him. I watched one afternoon as she made an apple pie. Kneading away at the dough, rolling it out, cutting it into strips, lining the pie dish with it, slicing the apples, raining cinnamon upon them, packing them into the dish until it was full and wanting only the top crust.

She wondered at the beauty of flowers, the depth of the ocean, the height and blueness of the sky. And she fell in love with reading, treasuring every book she read and receiving ongoing words of encouragement from Octavius Joy.

"How is my favorite scholar today?" he would ask each time he saw her.

She was in his home from time to time. She grew familiar with the dining room, parlour, drawing room, and kitchen, his study on the ground floor where he conducted business, and the wonderful staircase with a balustrade so broad that she might have walked up it almost as easily as on the stairs themselves.

But her favorite room—and it was Mr. Joy's favorite as well— was the library. It was a large room lit during the day by windows on the south and west walls and by lamps at night. There were comfortable chairs and an ornate carpet. But its most remarkable feature was shelves that stretched from floor to ceiling and were lined with books. Some were in fine leather-bound sets. Others had the appearance of having been collected here and there at different times.

"There are a great many books here, are there not?" Mr. Joy had said to Ruby on one of her visits when she was young.

"Yes, sir. I never saw so many."

"Someday, you shall read as many of them as you like. With a few, the back and cover are the best parts. But the insides are better where most are concerned."

Almost always, their conversations touched on reading. At age six, Ruby had given Mr. Joy an alphabet chart on which she painstakingly drew all twenty-six letters in an array of colours. On each of her birthdays, he gave her books commensurate with her reading skills.

"All people should be able to reap the harvest that is stored in books," he told her. "It is through reading that one learns the wonders of the world, the mighty changes of time, and the name of the street that one is walking on. The demon of ignorance and poverty feeds on illiteracy. I will not stand for it."

On Ruby's sixteenth birthday, Mr. Joy sent word that he would like to see her at his home. She went, not knowing what to expect. He met her at the front door and brought her to his study.

A large bay window looked out onto a bright flower garden. There was a tea service on a silver tray and a plate of nectarines beside another plate that was filled with sponge cakes.

Mr. Joy gave Ruby a small box wrapped in red paper. She opened it. There was a necklace inside. A gold necklace with a sparkling ruby.

"As befits your name," he told her. "And now, there is some-thing else that I would like to discuss."

Ruby waited, uncertain as to what would come next.

"You are a young woman of special ability," Mr. Joy continued. "You have been given much, and you have much to offer. I would like you to consider working at the learning center. You will be paid a salary. You would be a teacher."

Of all the things Ruby had dreamed for her future, she had never dreamed of being a teacher.

"But only men teach," she said.

Octavius Joy smiled. "I cannot think of a single reason why a young woman is not qualified to teach. Can you?"

"No, sir. It is just, I have not heard of it being commonly done."

"Nonsense. Mothers teach their children to read all the time."

One month after her sixteenth birthday, Ruby began work at the learning center, assisting older, more experienced teachers. Never have students received more diligent, kindhearted instruction.

Some of them came to the learning center, anxious and frightened. Others pretended to be rougher than they really were. Ruby greeted each one with a smile and told them how happy she was that they were there. Her manner and gender made learning a more comfortable experience for women. Men wanted to be in her presence. Children adored her.

There was a patience in her face that led those who had been anxious to take readily to her. And she had words of encouragement for everyone.

A young man about twenty years of age had a laugh that was more cheerful than intelligent. Given the fact that he had been a slow boy for the first two decades of his life, it seemed unlikely that he would ever become a fast one. Indeed, at his first session, he held his paper with the alphabet on it upside down, which seemed to suit his convenience as well as if he had been holding it right side up.

"You must never belittle yourself," Ruby told him.

A stout bald gentleman with a cheerful face had a tendency to stand with his hands in his pockets and whistle while admiring the writing on the wall as one might contemplate a painting by Rembrandt.

"Your letters are beautiful," Ruby complimented after he struggled through his first few letters.

And to a girl of twelve who had tears of frustration in her eyes: "Queen Victoria, who sits upon the throne, began her learning with the same alphabet. She started with 'A' just like you. And it took her quite a while to work her royal way to 'Z'."

⁂

Then tragedy.

In Christopher's fortieth year, he began to feel pain and weakness that should not have been in a man his age.

There is a dread condition that prepares its victims for death. A disease that medicine has never cured and wealth has never warded off. It is an illness that sometimes moves in giant strides and sometimes at a sluggish pace but, whether quick or slow, is certain. A condition in which the outcome of the struggle between body and soul is so sure that, day by day, the mortal part of the sufferer withers away and the spirit, feeling death at hand, welcomes the end as a lightening load.

Ruby comforted herself with the hope that Christopher would recover, as he answered with a quiet smile each day that he felt better than the day before. But he continued to grow thinner, and his eyes sank deeply into his face until his look was that of the gaunt starving man I had seen when he and Ruby first stood in the cold outside my bakery window.

Marie asked often if there was something she could do for him. Christopher's answer was always the same.

"Nothing."

For a while, he was strong enough to walk about with Ruby supporting him on her arm. They visited places that they remembered from the past. Each one brought some earlier event to mind, and they would linger in the sunlight with a word, a laugh . . . a fear.

One walk led them to the churchyard where Ruby's mother was buried.

"Sometimes when I look at you," Christopher told Ruby, "I see your mother's spirit in your eyes. When I die, I should like to be buried as near to her grave as they can make my own."

Ruby gave her promise, holding his hand.

"I shall never be an old man. But if I could know before I die that you will grow up to be happy and that you will come and look upon my grave from time to time, not with tears but with a smile, I could take my leave contented. You are a wonderful young woman. I love you as a daughter. I have nothing to regret but that I will not be here longer for you."

Each day, Ruby and Marie put Christopher in a chair by the window so he could feel the fresh air. But all the air that there is in the world and all the winds that blow could not have brought new life to him.

The little home in which they had laughed for years while planning happy futures was now somber.

"You are spending too much time by my bedside," Christopher told Ruby. "It troubles me that I am burdening you."

"I am here because I want to be. My earliest memories are of you sitting by my side and caring for me in a hovel that was a home only because you were there. I have known no father but you. Never was a parent more kind to a child than you have been to me."

She had never loved him more dearly than she did now. But she knew that hope was gone and death was closing fast. He could no longer move from room to room without assistance. He was so emaciated that it was hard to look upon him.

"Come close so you can hear me," Christopher told Ruby one night. "You are as good as any person of wealth and rank in the eyes of God. And in my eyes, you are better. My greatest fear after the death of your mother was that I should die and there would be no one to look after you. Now I know that you are loved and well cared for."

Soon, he could no longer leave his bed, so it was moved beside the window. When the rays of the sun shimmered on the wall, Christopher knew that it was day. When the reflection died away and a deepening gloom crept into the room, he knew that it was night. More and more often, he lay still without talking until a word from Ruby or Marie brightened his face for a moment. Then the light would dim.

"I can do nothing for myself," he said. "Once, I could, but that time is gone. For ten and three years, this has been my happy home. I shall leave it soon, but do not be sorry for me, dear Ruby. You have made my life very happy."

It is a dreadful thing to wait for death, to know that hope is gone and recovery is impossible. I have seen many people die. Little babies and great strong men. I know when death is coming.

"He will have every comfort possible," Ruby, Marie, and I pledged. "And one of us will always be with him. He shall not die alone."

Death came on a crisp autumn afternoon when the ground was coloured by fallen leaves and many more hung upon the trees in tints of red and gold.

"Come close," Christopher said to Ruby. "I want to see your face one more time."

"Do not leave us. Please do not leave."

"I will be with the angels. I have had the most blissful rest today, better than sleep. And such a pleasant happy dream. I almost think that, if I could rise from this bed, I would not do so. Someday, we will meet again. I feel the truth of that so strongly that I can bear to part from you now."

His eyes were bright, but their light was of Heaven, not earth. He moved his lips, but no sound came. Then he fell into a deep slumber from which there was no waking.

There was a burial service. Christopher was laid to rest in the churchyard near his sister's grave. Thinking of him now, many years later, I fancy him standing before me with Ruby at his side. She is three years old. They are shivering in the cold. She is clutching his hand, and her blue eyes are raised toward his face with love and wonder.

Book 2

CHAPTER 4

Edwin's parents married for love.

John Chatfield was a teacher in Portsea, giving him a status in life midway between England's upper and lower classes. Rebecca Hyde was the governess in a family that Mr. Chatfield visited from time to time. Mr. Chatfield took notice of Miss Hyde and paid an increasing amount of attention to her. Eventually, he proposed marriage and she accepted. Two years later, in 1832, Edwin was born.

As Edwin was breathing the first breaths of his life, his mother was breathing her last.

"Is there nothing that can be done?" John Chatfield begged.

The doctor shook his head. Death was at her pillow.

Edwin's mother reached weakly toward the infant and, in a faint voice, pled, "Let me hold my child."

The doctor placed the infant in her arms. With a trembling hand, she caressed her son's cheek, pressed his tiny hand against her mouth, and imprinted her lips upon his forehead. The shadow of a smile crossed her face. Then her breathing stopped, and her soul drifted out upon the dark eternal sea that rolls round the world.

The doctor chafed her breast and hands, but the flow of her blood had ceased.

She died like a child that had gone to sleep. Edwin would never again know a mother's loving touch. He would never hear a mother's voice singing to him. He could only dream in future years of a mother's arms round him. But for a moment, she had loved him.

As a young boy, Edwin had a solemn sweetness and a calm shy smile. When twilight fell, he would walk outside with his father, look up at the sky, and wait for the first clear shining star. Whichever of them saw it first—and almost always, it was Edwin—would cry out, "I see a star!"

A sketch in ink of Edwin's mother hung in the home. The graceful head of a pretty woman was all that he knew of her looks. Once, he asked his father if he had met his mother before she died, for he could not remember if he had or not.

"You met her one time when you were very young," his father told him.

"Was she happy when she saw me?"

"Her whole face lit up in a smile when she saw you. And she said to you, 'Edwin, I love you.'"

"I don't remember."

"It was a long time ago."

"Where did she go?"

"Come and sit beside me, and I will tell you a story. Once upon a time, there was a wonderful mother. She had a son named Edwin and dearly loved him. But she was taken very ill and died and was buried in the ground where the grass and flowers and trees grow. No one will see her again. But she loved both of us very much."

Once, Edwin asked his father if he could take the picture of his mother off the wall and hold it. Then he kissed her on the cheek.

"I feel bad for everyone that they have to die," he said.

Childhood is a time for a hopeful vision of things that are so real in one's imagination that few realities achieved thereafter are stronger. Edwin grew up with the dreams of childhood and airy fables that are so good to be believed when young and so good to be remembered when older.

He often asked questions beyond his age about the order of the world. His mind was always full of thought. At church on Sundays, rather than listen to the sermons that droned on and on, he would look at the pulpit and imagine what a good place it would be to play in and what a fine castle it would make with another boy coming up the stairs to attack and Edwin throwing the velvet cushion with tassels down on his head.

He was taught to read at an early age. He and his father read Hans Christian Andersen's fairy tales together. Then came Robin Hood in Sherwood Forest and Robinson Crusoe standing alone with dog and hatchet, surveying his domain. When the wind blew at night and rain was driving against the windows, Edwin sat by the fire, reading of shipwrecks and knights and civilizations long gone. His books were like friends. He read them over and over. They were treasures to him.

Because his father was a teacher, Edwin entered school at an early age. The other boys were from wealthier families.

"What class are you?" one of them asked.

"I am an Englishman," Edwin told him.

He and the other boys studied the lineage of the kings and queens of England from the Normans through the Plantagenets, Tudors, Stuarts, and Hanoverians.

Queen Victoria, Edwin learned, was born in 1819. Her father died one year later, whilst George III sat upon the throne. Three kings of England died thereafter, two of them leaving no legitimate children. On 20 June 1837, at the age of eighteen, Victoria ascended to the throne.

Edwin's father instilled in him the belief that it is a great satisfaction to know that you have done the best you can. As a schoolboy, Edwin was far beyond his peers in learning. He was handsomely formed with the grace of youth and a serious but engaging manner. The other boys liked and respected him. He had the aura of one who would be successful someday.

As Edwin grew older, his character was marked by sincerity, constancy, and candor. Few grown men were as thorough as he in his work or as trustworthy. With each year that passed, he grew more and more handsome. There was majesty in his eyes.

While in school, Edwin had thought of becoming a teacher. But his father wanted a more prosperous life for him. "I should like it," he told Edwin, "if you were to become a man of business."

A chain of referrals and introductions followed. Edwin, it was promised, would do credit to any employer who brought him on. In 1850, at age eighteen, he travelled by coach from Portsea to London to meet with a man named Alexander Murd.

Murd was a wealthy coal merchant with mines in Yorkshire and Lancashire. He had been born to wealth and, having received a substantial inheritance, married a larger one. His financial holdings included enough shares of stock to be on the Boards of Direction of several companies.

Murd's office was in a building entered by passing through a courtyard that was shut off from the street by a high wall and strong gate. A brass plate that held his name was affixed to the front door.

Edwin was brought into Murd's private room.

Murd rose from his desk and extended his hand. He was about forty-five years of age, handsome and elegantly dressed. They shook hands, and Murd commented favorably on the young man's references. Then Edwin sat, and Murd began to question him about his past and his goals for the future. Once he had learned what he wanted to know, the conversation shifted.

"I am a man of business," Murd told Edwin. "No more, no less. But it is an important business that contributes to the strength and grandeur of England. At the start of the eighteenth century, three million tons of coal were produced annually in England. A century later, the number was ten million. This year, seventy million tons of coal will be extracted from the ground. Coal is the lifeblood of our nation. It fuels factories and warms homes. Railroads and ships are dependent upon it."

As they talked, Murd weighed Edwin's appearance and manner. The young man had a keen mind and a gracious way about him. Nothing in his attire could have been changed to his advantage except for a finer grade of cloth. His expression was one of readiness to be questioned and to answer straight. He was, Murd noted, remarkably self-possessed for one so young. Indeed, there was a grace about him that a British Lord might not have been able to teach his son in forty years.

Murd very much wanted to employ him.

"Enterprise, careful planning, and effort are the keys to success," he told Edwin. "I am a careful man. I know my affairs thoroughly and expect that you will do the same. You are to be in the office each morning at nine o'clock. And better before than after."

Working for Murd required that Edwin move from Portsea to London. He found lodging in small but comfortable chambers that were plainly furnished and nicely kept.

Murd had no partner in his business, only subordinates. Numerous men were employed in the field to ensure that his mining operations functioned properly. Land likely to bear coal was identified and purchased. The coal was extracted from the ground by miners. Then it was sold and transported throughout England.

The London office was small in contrast to the total number of company employees. The staff in London, in addition to Edwin, consisted of an accountant, two clerks, a secretary, and office boy. The accountant—a tall angularly made man named Arthur Abbott—held rank over the others. His complexion was so pale, save for a red eruption here and there, that he looked as though he had been put away in a lumber closet twenty years before and someone had just found him.

Murd had a somewhat haughty manner. A solemn hush prevailed among the staff each morning as he passed through the outer office. When it was chill outside, the office boy was upon his heel to take his coat and hat on the instant of arrival.

Men of business came to the office in a steady stream. Murd had mastered all the points of their game. He studied their play and registered their cards in his mind. He was crafty in finding out what positions they held, but never betrayed his own hand.

Edwin was as punctual as the sun in keeping his hours. He blended steadiness with industriousness and determination. Unlike many young men who dash through their tasks with a certain distinction but in a less than thoughtful manner, he fully considered the implications of each step he took. His commitment to understanding the length and breadth and depth of every piece of work entrusted to him was as impressive as his dispatch in accomplishing it. He was as far from intrusive as an employee could be. Yet nothing less than a complete understanding and mastery of each assignment satisfied him.

Also, there was within Edwin an inborn power of attraction that led people to like him.

Time passed. Edwin turned from eighteen to nineteen, then twenty. In autumn of 1852, a chance encounter—at least, Edwin believed it was chance—led to his meeting Alexander Murd's daughter.

Murd was working from his home that day and sent word to the office that he would like Edwin to visit to discuss a business matter. Edwin travelled by omnibus to Grosvenor Square—the aristocratic part of London where Murd lived—and presented himself at the door.

The house was spacious and grandly furnished. Murd was rich. How rich, Edwin did not know. But it was clear from his home that he had amassed a fortune large enough to satisfy several wealthy men for a lifetime.

A servant led Edwin to Murd's study. The walls were lined with engravings, each one representing a different month of the year. Murd sat behind an elegant desk fashioned from mahogany with leather and inlaid wood covering the top. He spoke with Edwin about several transactions that were being negotiated. Their meeting lasted less than an hour. As they were concluding, there was a knock on the door and a young woman about Edwin's age entered. She had rounded cheeks, a pointed nose, and disagreeably sharp eyes. Murd introduced her as his daughter, Isabella.

Isabella, who smelled of scented soap, looked at Edwin approvingly. They exchanged pleasantries. Then the same servant who had escorted Edwin to the study escorted him back to the front door.

The following day, Murd called Edwin into his private room at work.

"Mrs. Murd and I have invited several couples to our home for dinner on Saturday evening. My daughter has suggested that you join us."

The invitation, Edwin understood, was both an honour and a command. Over the next few days, he wondered what he should wear, whether he should bring a gift—flowers, perhaps—and what the rules of conduct would be.

The evening at Murd's home began in the parlour, which was elegantly furnished in burgundy and gold. The other guests were a bank director, the chairman of a public company, and their wives.

The bank director—a man named Maurice Allard—had as much hair on his head as an egg and was grossly overweight. The influence of good living had expanded his face so that its curves extended far beyond the limits originally assigned to them. His chin had a shape best described by prefixing the word "double" to it.

The chairman of the public company—Frederick Haight—was closely shaved and expensively clothed, glossy and crisp like a new banknote. He laughed in a metallic sort of way and had a half-smile that was not at all expressive of good humour.

Neither man, it seemed from the conversation, was likely to make a mistake against his own financial interest in any matter over which he presided. Nor was Edwin inclined to assume kindness on their part.

Isabella followed Edwin constantly with her eyes. She was expensively dressed, but her clothes and jewelry amounted to little more than the polishing of an unattractive surface.

After an hour in the parlour, Murd led his guests to the dining room. Candles burned in elegant silver candlesticks, in decorative sconces, and on an ornate glass chandelier that hung from above. Ancestral portraits on the walls proclaimed, "Each of us was a passing reality and left this coloured shadow as a remembrance of who we were."

Murd and his wife sat at opposite ends of the table. There was a politeness and consideration in their behaviour toward one another, but it was rather cold and formal.

Edwin was paired with Isabella.

Dinner was gracefully served. There was a dish of fish, then choice mutton and a pair of roast stuffed fowl, with clean plates, clean knives, and clean forks for each course.

Maurice Allard ate with the delicacy of a hungry pig that had been shut up by mistake in the grain area of a brewery overnight.

Frederick Haight spoke proudly of his son, saying, "The very first word he learned to spell was 'gold.' And the first, after he advanced to two syllables, was 'money.'"

At one point, the conversation turned to an act of Parliament that prohibited boys under the age of ten and all women from working underground in mines.

"The legislation is misguided," Murd offered. "All it accomplishes is to deprive families of the money that they need to survive."

"The miners are like rats that burrow in and out of holes that they have dug into the ground," Isabella said scornfully. "We only hear of them when there is trouble. It would be better if the coal came out of the ground without them."

"They are God's children," Edwin told her.

"They have yet to learn that human beings should live differently from cattle," Isabella pressed.

"Perhaps if they were educated."

"I am not friendly to what is called general education," Murd interjected. "I believe it is necessary that the labouring classes be taught to know their position and to conduct themselves accordingly."

"And I believe, respectfully, sir, that all men and women are of common origin and deserving of the opportunity for happiness and respect."

"If I wish for a lecture on morality," Frederick Haight interjected, directing his remark to Edwin, "I shall go to church. You are a nice young man, but you are hopelessly naive."

"I am teaching him the ways of business," Murd assured his guest.

"If everyone were warm and well fed," Maurice Allard offered, "we should lose the satisfaction of admiring the fortitude with which a certain class of men and women bear cold and hunger. And if we were no better off than anybody else, what would become of our sense of gratitude?"

Dinner concluded with cake, cheese, and sliced oranges steeped in sugar, followed by a port wine that had been bottled a half-century before.

"I meant no harm by my comments," Edwin said to his host at evening's end.

"And you have done none. I would simply urge you to keep in mind that a man may have the softest heart in the world, but he and his family cannot live upon it."

The day after dining at Murd's, Edwin sent a note of thanks to his host:

Dear Mr. Murd,

Thank you for welcoming me into your home and sharing your family and friends so graciously with me. I am most appreciative.

Sincerest wishes,

Edwin

But in truth, the evening and particularly the conversation at dinner troubled Edwin.

Murd took pride in the notion that his business was essential to building the engines of society. He often assured Edwin that the young man had a promising career ahead of him. But Edwin was beginning to question whether he belonged in Murd's world.

He was not fond of Murd. Time and again, he saw his employer summon a look of easy charm when business required it. But as soon as the mask was no longer needed, it was gone from his face. Edwin wondered if there had ever been a time when a child's heart beat in his breast.

And he had a visceral dislike for Murd's daughter.

Isabella had a smile that reeked of insincerity. Her view of life had been formed in the mirror of the highly polished walnut and rosewood furnishings of her parents' home. She was unduly impressed with what she believed was her own superior breeding, a sentiment that she exhibited freely and with obvious condescension toward others. Her character was marked by numerous manifestations of having been spoiled by her father's wealth. When dining, she ate only the prime parts of meat, leaving the rest on her plate and asking for more prime parts if still hungry.

Looking in the mirror, Isabella saw not her real self but the reflection of some pleasant image that existed in her brain. After meeting Edwin at her parents' home, she came to the office fairly often, which he regarded as an unpleasant intrusion upon his working day. She was always flirtatious, touching his arm in a predatory manner. Edwin was guided in these encounters by politeness. But he would have preferred the embrace of a bear that smelled badly to her touch.

Miss Murd reasoned that she was beautiful and charming, and that her father was Edwin's master and had a great deal of money, all of which seemed to constitute a conclusive argument as to why Edwin should feel honoured by her attentions.

Murd's wife had given him only one daughter and no sons to

follow in his footsteps. He was not concerned about a husband for his daughter so much as he wanted a son-in-law to help run his business.

Some young men less scrupulous than Edwin might have encouraged Isabella's delusions. By virtue of whatever influence she had upon her father, she could render Edwin's future at work more promising if she were his friend. Edwin had no way of knowing the depth of her infatuation with him. Nor did he know that Isabella had asked her father if she could keep the note of thanks that Edwin had written after being in their home for dinner.

Another winter passed. Edwin continued to work diligently in the office. Owing to the long hours he kept, his social opportunities were limited. He read often in his spare time.

There was a loneliness in his life, an emptiness inside of him.

Then came a day in March. Winter had not yet turned to spring. But the sun was full up and there was activity in the streets. People hurried back and forth. Shop windows and doors were open. Labourers were at work, some hauling and delivering wares, others digging and building.

There was a sharp wind.

The wind was important to what followed.

Edwin was walking along a busy street when he saw a gust of wind blow a man's hat off his head.

There are very few moments in a man's life when he feels as silly as when he is in pursuit of his own hat. The best way to catch it is to keep up with it, get gradually before it, bend down, seize it, and stick it firmly on your head, smiling pleasantly all the time as though you thought it was as good a joke as everyone who was watching. But that was difficult here inasmuch as the man was on the stout side and a trifle clumsy. He puffed, the wind puffed, and the hat rolled on as merrily as a porpoise in a strong tide.

Eventually, the man lost sight of his hat and was staring about in all directions but the right one. He was on the verge of accepting his loss when Edwin, with a few lively steps, accomplished what the man could not. Then, hat in hand, he walked toward the hat's rightful owner.

The man was wearing a dark-blue coat. His chin rested in the folds of an old-fashioned white neckcloth, not a stiff starched cravat. He was older than Edwin had thought at first. A good seventy years of age. But there was something so engaging about his appearance that it was a pleasure to look at him. A merry smile and kindhearted expression lit up his face. His eyes were twinkling and honest.

"I believe that this is yours, sir," Edwin said, handing the man his hat.

The older man looked at Edwin approvingly.

"I am much obliged for your kindness. Perhaps I could buy you tea to thank you for your effort."

Edwin was a bit hungry. And he liked the older man's manner.

"I would like that, sir. Thank you."

"Very well then. There is a café on the next block." The man extended his hand in greeting. "My name is Octavius Joy."

"And I am Edwin Chatfield."

Soon, they were seated opposite one another. Octavius Joy ordered tea, cakes, rolls, butter, and jam for two. Then their conversation began in earnest. He at once showed an interest in Edwin, asking his age and the circumstances of his being in London.

"And your parents?"

"My mother died giving life to me. My father is a teacher."

"A noble profession. Education is a great thing, a very great thing."

"I think often that teaching might be a better path for me than the one I have chosen."

"You are young. There is time for you to find your calling."

As they talked, Octavius Joy studied Edwin's face. He prided himself on being able to discern a man's character by listening to his words and studying his eyes. He liked the way this young man carried himself. There was an aura of integrity about him. His eyes were those of one who trusted others and was worthy of trust.

"This is an uncommon young man," Octavius Joy told himself. "A good one, I am sure. It is a pity that his mother could not see him as he is now. It would have made her happy and proud."

They talked a bit more about education.

"The future of England is dependent upon a better educated population," Octavius Joy said. "From the beginning of time, only a tiny portion of all the people who ever lived have been able to read. There was a time when that did not matter. But it matters now. I believe very strongly that all people should be taught to read and write. It is a passion of mine."

Then he told Edwin about the learning center.

"I think that you would approve of its mission and how it works. Would you like to accompany me there?"

He paused, weighing his next words.

"And there is a young lady there that you might like to meet."

❦

Five months had passed since Christopher's death. Ruby gave thanks for the years that she had been blessed to have her uncle in her life. Still, she missed him.

Christopher lay buried beneath a tree in a quiet churchyard

corner. In late afternoon, the church spire cast a long shadow on his grave. It was comforting for Ruby to think of him as being in Heaven. But in his worldly form, he rested here, separated from the living by a few boards and a little earth.

Winter came and brought with it more than the usual share of cold heavy rain. Ruby visited the churchyard often, reading the names upon the stones, wondering who those at rest might have been and whom they had left behind. When the church bell struck on the hour, she fancied that Christopher was speaking to her.

She wished that she had asked him more about her mother. It was a subject that he had been reluctant to talk about. Now she and Christopher were parted, never to meet again on this side of eternity. Perhaps someday she would see him and her mother in Heaven.

It was a bright windy March afternoon. The walls of the learning center were ornamented with illustrations from Mother Goose, fairy tales from the Brothers Grimm, and popular classics.

A small dark-haired boy came straggling in and, after him, a red-headed lad and, after him, a girl with flaxen hair. Soon, a dozen chairs were occupied by boys and girls with heads of every colour but grey.

There was a lesson. The children hung on Ruby's every word, their bright faces coming alive. Then writing time began, and the children concentrated on their letters. Ruby walked about, looking over each child's shoulder, praising an up-stroke here, a down-stroke there. Where correction was necessary, she suggested that the child look at how a particular letter was formed on the wall and take it for a model.

"Can you read Dickens?" one of the boys asked.

"I can," Ruby told him. "And you will too someday."

Then Ruby saw Octavius Joy standing in the entrance to the learning center. A young man, perhaps two years older than she, was with him.

The young man was handsome with an earnest face. His hair was dark with a slight inclination to wave. His eyes fired up as though their depths were stirred by something wonderful.

A sensation that Ruby had never known before swept through her. And she felt that her life was about to change.

CHAPTER 5

Octavius Joy made the introduction between them.

"I have known Miss Spriggs since she was three years old. I have known Mr. Chatfield since shortly before eleven o'clock this morning."

"Are you a scholar?" Ruby asked, for Edwin had the look of one.

"I am tolerably educated."

Octavius Joy explained to Ruby the circumstances of the wind, his hat, and meeting Edwin.

"I suggested that Mr. Chatfield come to the learning center. He tells me that he has an interest in teaching people to read."

"There is no greater good than teaching one's fellow man to read," Edwin offered.

"And women," Ruby corrected.

"And women. Forgive me for not expressing myself with greater precision."

Ruby had never seen a face as handsome as Edwin's. Not even in pictures.

"She has a pretty face," Edwin thought to himself. "A very pretty face. An unusually pretty face."

He could no more have removed his eyes from Ruby's face than he could have flown to the moon.

"What you see in this room," Octavius Joy said, addressing Edwin, "is England's future. Knowledge is becoming more widespread. There is a move toward more education. Every person in this room feels an attraction to the dignity and utility of learning."

All of this occurred on a Wednesday. Given Edwin's schedule at work, it was agreed that he would return to the learning center on Saturday, a day on which the great majority of those in attendance would be grown men and women. Once he understood the methods of instruction, he would assist in teaching.

It was apparent soon after Edwin began that he was a natural teacher. He had a gift for explaining clearly and also a caring quality about him. In less than a month, every person at the learning center was his friend.

In the past, Ruby had taught each week from Monday through Friday. It did not go unnoticed that, after Edwin's arrival, she began to appear at the learning center on Saturdays as well. Mr. Chatfield and Miss Spriggs seemed to have an affinity for one another, exchanging glances and dancing with their eyes.

Edwin remained conflicted regarding his employment. All the while, his education in the coal business continued. He attended meetings in which Murd negotiated purchase orders from buyers, and he became familiar with the ways and cost of shipping coal throughout England. He read geologists' reports as to where the richest veins might be found, and was a pleasant presence when called upon by Murd to sit at lunch with business associates.

"The other men in the company are in positions that are right for them and shall rise no higher," Murd told Edwin. "You have a more promising future."

Those words, however well intended they might have been, were not reassuring. Edwin's dislike for his employer was growing. He sensed a dark spirit within him. Some men live with the primary, if not sole, object of enriching and then further enriching themselves. Avarice is their vice. Murd was one of them.

The secrets of Murd's domain were in the books and papers locked in a cabinet in his private room at the office. From time to time, Edwin saw him take a small key from his pocket, unlock a drawer in his desk in which there was another key, and use the second key to open the cabinet. At times, Edwin wondered what secrets were in the cabinet. Other times, he did not want to know.

One thing, he did know. A dependence on Alexander Murd would likely embitter his life. "How strange it is," Edwin thought, "to be never satisfied, never at rest, always reaching for an infinite number of coins."

And there was another thing that Edwin was certain of. The least pleasant part of his employment was the appearance in the office from time to time of Isabella Murd.

Isabella took unseemly pride in her family background and considered her lineage superior to that of virtually everyone else in England. She talked often about money, which she said was better than anything, and had a perpetually sullen look upon her face. One afternoon, she spent a full thirty minutes telling Edwin about her maid, who, according to the recitation, prepared Isabella's clothes for dressing, arranged her hair, assisted in dressing her, sat up for her when she went out at night, assisted in undressing her, put away her jewels, kept her wardrobe in repair, washed her lace and linens, and was up early each morning to prepare Isabella's breakfast tray.

Given Edwin's feelings, he regarded it as a particularly unfortunate turn of events when Murd summoned him to his office one afternoon and, with Isabella present, informed Edwin that he was to take Isabella to the opera the following evening.

"Mrs. Murd and I have decided to give you our tickets. Our coachman will be at your disposal."

"I must be honest with you," Edwin protested. "Your kind offer is very much appreciated, but there are others who would enjoy the opera more than I. The spoken word appeals to me. The same words, sung in a language that I do not understand, do not."

Murd was insistent.

It was an unpleasant night. Edwin disliked opera, though not so much as he disliked Isabella. On the evening of the performance, her gown was too bright an orange and the ribbons in her hair too intensely green. She began the conversation in the carriage on the way to the opera by talking about various men who had pursued her.

"Perhaps you could keep a register of these attachments with notations regarding the dates of each," Edwin suggested. "You could list them as though they were reigns of the kings and queens of England."

Ignoring the comment, Isabella began to discourse on her family's wealth.

"My father's fortune is large. I have been brought up with the expectation that I shall always be rich. From early childhood, I have travelled in the most polite and best circles of society."

When they left the carriage to enter the opera hall, Isabella took Edwin's arm. He did not like the feel of it. Nor did he like the opera, although he found it less disagreeable than the sound of Isabella's voice.

"Do you think that I particularly like you?" Isabella asked during the carriage ride home.

"I have not asked myself that question."

"Ask yourself the question now."

"You act at times as though you do."

"And is my fondness returned?"

Ask no questions, and you will be told no lies, Edwin thought but did not say.

"I think that you are a very nice woman. And I admire your father greatly."

"My father speaks quite well of you. He says that you have a unique ability to draw others over to your side. That is a great asset in business."

"Sometimes I wonder if my life would not be better spent as a teacher, helping others who would not otherwise learn to read and write."

"Someday, perhaps, you will make your fortune in business and use the money to pay for others to go to school. Think of all the laughing little children you could make happy."

There was sarcasm in her voice.

Shortly after Edwin attended the opera, he sent a brief note of thanks to Isabella. It seemed the proper thing to do:

Dear Miss Murd,

Thank you for the pleasure of your company this past Saturday evening. You have brought the most beautiful music into my life.

Then, with a sincerity matching her own, he added:

I envision a future with laughing children learning to read and write.

Very truly yours,

Edwin

He did not realize at the time the extent of her delusions.

Several days later, Murd called Edwin into his private office.

"My daughter tells me that she fancies you, and that your attentions toward her are serious. I approve."

In that moment, Edwin made a vow to himself. He would never again accept a social engagement with Isabella. Not even if the price to be paid was the loss of his employment.

Meanwhile, Edwin's visits to the learning center continued. Every Saturday, Ruby was there when he arrived. "You know, do you not," another of the instructors told her, "that he comes here to see you. It is clear on his face. The moment he enters, his eyes seek you out."

She hoped that was true. Time glided swiftly and cheerfully when she was with Edwin. Hours seemed like minutes in his presence. And he was as devoted to teaching as she was.

"To be illiterate and see other people read and write when you cannot," Edwin told her one day; "to see the postmen deliver letters and to be blind to all that is in them; to walk through the streets in utter darkness as to the meaning of those mysterious symbols over shops, on shop doors, and in windows. That is the curse of illiteracy."

No moment in the learning center moved Edwin more than the sight one afternoon of a man poring hard over a tattered newspaper. One year earlier, Edwin knew, the man's wife had come to the learning center and spoken with Ruby.

"My husband does not know that I am here," she had said. "He is a good man. I would not shame him for the world. But he cannot read or write, and I wish that he were able to."

"He should come here," Ruby told her. "And you should come too."

Now a tear coursed down the man's cheek as he completed reading an article from the newspaper aloud for the class.

"I can read," he said. "The world opens up before me."

Then came a day in May. At the close of instruction, Edwin lingered after the students and other instructors had left the learning center.

"I have a gift for you," he told Ruby.

And he handed her a book.

Ruby stared at the cover. Blue decorated with a gilt wreath and words in gold: *The Adventures of Oliver Twist*.

"It is one of my favorites," Edwin said. "I have inscribed it for you."

She turned to the title page:

For Miss Ruby Spriggs,

Children who cannot read are like gardens
without sunlight.
We can all do good if we try.

Fondly,
Edwin Chatfield

Had the gift been diamonds, it would not have meant as much to her. Ruby had never been so happy in her entire life. Edwin looked more handsome to her than ever before. Their faces were very close to one another.

You may kiss me if you like, Ruby thought.

"Dickens is meant to be read aloud," Edwin said. "Perhaps we could meet again tomorrow."

"I would like that very much, Mr. Chatfield."

"I would prefer it if you call me Edwin."

"I would be happy to if you will call me Ruby."

The following morning, Ruby rose with the sun. A sun that brought the hope and freshness of a new day. It burst with equal ray through the stained glass windows in lofty cathedrals and paper-mended windows in crumbling hovels.

In Marie's bakery, the sun seemed particularly bright. Ruby had suggested that Edwin meet her there at the start of their day together. I was present with Marie. By Ruby's invitation, of course.

Ruby was dressed in the prettiest colours that she could muster. Edwin arrived at the invited hour of ten o'clock. It pleased me to see them side by side. There was a kindred spirit between them.

Edwin had an honest face, which to me is the best kind of good looks. His joy in being with Ruby was clear, as was hers to be with him. Her eyes had never glowed more brightly. Never had there been such a beautiful colour in her cheeks. She gazed at Edwin with the eagerness of a young woman in love for the first time.

Marie served coffee, pastries, muffins, butter, and strawberry jam. Afterward, Ruby and Edwin left the bakery together and walked out onto the street. He was speaking with his head turned toward her. She was looking at his face and saw nothing else.

They were, Marie and I agreed, extremely fond of one another. I believe that Ruby would have committed herself to mastering geometry at that moment if she had thought it would please Edwin.

After they left the bakery, Ruby and Edwin went to the park and read aloud the beginning of *Oliver Twist*.

"There are fifty-two more chapters," Ruby said when the first chapter was done.

"Then I hope we will spend the next fifty-two Sundays together."

The sky was beautiful. There was a soft stirring wind. They strolled through Covent Garden market, smelling the fruits and flowers, looking at pineapples and melons, catching glimpses down side avenues of old women seated on inverted baskets, shelling peas. Ducks and fowls with long necks lay stretched out in pairs, ready for cooking. There were silvery fish stalls with a moonlight look about their stock except for the ruddy lobsters.

Edwin drew Ruby's arm through his. The touch of his arm was like no other she had known. She would never forget the rapid beating of her heart in that moment.

It is remarkable how much two young people in love will find to talk about. Their conversation flowed easily.

At one point, they talked of family.

"My ancestry is very common," Ruby acknowledged.

"That is true of all men and women, including the Queen, if one goes back far enough in time."

"Have you a memory of your mother?"

Edwin shook his head.

"Her eyes closed upon the light of the world when mine opened to it. There was a drawing of her on the wall in our home. Beyond that, I know her only by her grave."

"My mother was a beautiful woman," Ruby offered. "My uncle told me that it was so. But there is no likeness of her. I believe that I have a memory of her singing to me when I was very young. But I am not sure."

"It must have been difficult to grow up without mother or father."

"There was never a better father to a child that my uncle Christopher was to me. Marie has given me more love than many a mother gives to her children. And Antonio is a very good uncle."

Two young people with magic in the air. The butterflies fluttered more gaily than Ruby or Edwin had seen them before. The birds sang more beautifully than they had ever heard them sing. A gentle breeze rustled about as if saying, "How are you, my dears? I have come all this way to salute you."

After a stop for cheese and bread, they walked on. They passed a chemist's shop with glowing bottles of different shapes and sizes in the window. They stood outside a tailor shop, commenting upon how the waistcoat patterns always appeared impeccably stylish when on a mannequin, yet never looked quite the same when worn by the purchaser.

Then a monstrous dark cloud appeared.

Isabella Murd stood before them on the street, unmoved by the bright sunny spirit of the day except insofar as it had spared her the trouble of carrying an umbrella.

If Ruby lived to be one hundred years old, she would never forget the look on Isabella's face. A rabid wolf would have been more enticing. Look at this young lady on Edwin's arm, the look said. I hate her.

Edwin, after a moment's pause, introduced them.

"This is Isabella Murd, the daughter of my employer. And this is my friend, Ruby Spriggs."

Isabella stared at Ruby with scornful jealous eyes.

"Ruby is such an interesting name," she said contemptuously.

"Thank you, ma'am. Isabella is a beautiful name, too."

There was little further conversation.

"She does not like me," Ruby told Edwin after they and Isabella had parted. "Not at all."

"Let her fly away in a high wind on a broomstick," Edwin responded.

Ruby laughed. She and Edwin walked on.

The glory of the departing sun set the broad sky on fire. The light of day faded. The sombre hues of evening closed upon them. There was a lamplighter and two lengthening lines of fire that stretched parallel down the street until blending together in the distance. The sweet scent of honeysuckle floated through the air. Never had the moon risen with a more wondrous radiance over London than it did that night.

At the close of their day together, Edwin walked Ruby home and kissed her hand at the door. She was certain that she would never be kissed so magnificently ever again unless, perhaps, it was another time by Edwin. She prayed that she would always love her life as much as she did now. Before sleeping, she sat on her bed, held the book that Edwin had given to her, and stared at the inscription that flowed from his hand.

It had been the happiest day of her life. Happy walk, happy parting, happy dreams.

Outside Ruby's window, the twilight deepened into night. Edwin walked home along streets that were bright in the silvery light of the moon. Stars twinkled. He knew the names that science had given the constellations, but they had deeper meaning to him now.

"There is a spell upon me," Edwin thought. "This is what it is like to be in love."

CHAPTER 6

Ruby went to sleep with Edwin's kiss light on her hand.

For the rest of her life, she would think of love's awakening in association with that day. The world had seemed as though it were made fresh and new just for her and Edwin that morning. For hours on end, it had been hard to know whether she was awake or in a dream.

She would always remember the moment when Edwin bade her goodnight at the bakery door. When they had parted, there was such a beautiful expression in his eyes. He was in her prayers and in her sleep that night. London itself was different now from what she had known before.

Ruby went to the learning center as usual on Monday. Marie invited me for dinner that evening. Ruby met me at the bakery door.

"I have a great secret to tell you," she said.

"Shall I try to guess?"

She blushed.

"I wonder who it can be about," said I.

"It is about . . ." Ruby said in a whisper . . . "It is about Edwin."

"And what about Edwin?"

"Of course, I admire him very much."

"And?"

"And I am rather fond of him."

"You are extremely fond of him."

She blushed some more.

"I never told you that."

"You do not tell me when you cut your hair either. But I have the intelligence to perceive it."

Her beautiful young face was growing redder by the moment. I laughed, and she embraced me.

"And I believe that I am in love with Edwin. Do you think he likes me?"

"He more than likes you. It is as clearly written on his face as it is on yours. The only difference is that he blushes less."

I was right, of course.

Edwin had never known the worth of his heart before. Walking to the office on Monday morning, he found himself reading signs above shop doors without remembering what they said and staring into windows at things he did not see. Saturday next, when he and Ruby would be together at the learning center, could not come soon enough. And then they would have another Sunday together.

"I have never seen a smile such as hers," Edwin told himself. "Nor eyes that sparkled so, or a waist that so enticed a man to clasp the air involuntarily when thinking of twining his arm round it."

Isabella came to the office on Monday afternoon, as Edwin had feared she might.

"And who was that young lady I saw you with on the street?"

"Her name, as I told you when we met, is Ruby Spriggs."

"Where do you know her from?"

"She is a teacher at the learning center, where I give my time on Saturdays."

"Marriage and motherhood are the only satisfactory roles for women. That is, of course, for women of a decent class."

"Miss Spriggs's class is the same as mine. We are both citizens of England."

Isabella clasped her hands together with as much dignity as she could muster.

"I suppose that, for those who like plainness, she has a certain allure."

It was Edwin's hope that the conversation, as unpleasant as it was, would have the happy consequence of putting an end to Isabella's delusions with regard to his feelings toward her.

"Miss Spriggs is a young lady for whom I have great attachment and regard."

"I am sure. But consider how much more agreeable I can render your situation if I am your friend, and how much more disagreeable if I am your enemy."

No one knows until the time comes what depths are in others as to their capacity to do evil. There was an unspeakable jealousy in Isabella's breast. She hated Ruby with a vengeance and venality worthy of a member of the house of Murd.

As for her father . . .

One reason that men such as Alexander Murd do what they do is the thrill of playing the game. It is oxygen to them. Whether at a card table playing whist, in business dealings, or brutally intruding upon other people's lives, it is all the same to them. They are relentless and ruthless in pursuit of the win.

Murd was largely removed emotionally from his daughter's life. His relationships with his employees were strictly business in nature. He had no understanding of how delusional Isabella was, and truly believed that she and Edwin might someday marry. Also, making the assumption that he loved his daughter, he loved himself a great deal more.

A cold hard anger coursed through Murd's veins when Isabella came to him and recounted what she knew of Edwin and Ruby. Edwin was a valuable company asset. Murd did not want to lose his services over a lovers' quarrel. And because Murd was without a son, Edwin, as a possible son-in-law, might oversee the business someday.

Murd viewed the thought of Edwin and Ruby being together as an attack upon his family and himself. He resolved to bring all of his power to bear to crush whatever situation existed between them.

"Ruby Spriggs. That is the name I want to know about," Murd told his solicitor.

"What would you like to know?"

"Everything that can be learned from investigation. Her lineage. Whether there have been police matters concerning her or her family. Spare no expense. And I want this quickly done."

Four days later, at nine o'clock in the morning on Friday, Murd called Edwin into his private office and handed him an envelope.

"It is time to broaden your experience," Murd said. "This is a letter of introduction to Julian White, who is the head of our operations in Lancashire. It contains instructions regarding what he is to show and explain to you."

"Am I to be moved to Lancashire?"

Murd smiled benignly.

"Your home is in London. You are valued here. All that is intended is to broaden your understanding of the business."

"When would I go?"

"In two hours, by train from Euston Railway Station. Mr. Abbott has arranged for you to have fresh clothes and articles of personal grooming. They are waiting for you on his desk."

"How long would I be gone, sir?"

"One week at the most."

"I am afraid, sir, that it would be difficult for me to go."

Murd's face took on a questioning look.

"Why is that?"

"I have an engagement, sir. On Saturday and also on Sunday. Two hours is insufficient time for me to tell the other party of this change in plans."

"An easy matter to resolve. My coachman will deliver any message you wish."

"With all due respect, sir, I am not sure that your coachman can adequately express my feelings."

"Then put them in writing."

Murd handed Edwin a piece of stationery and an envelope.

"I have no desire to pry into personal matters. Write your message in private and seal it."

Pen in hand, Edwin began to write:

My Dearest Ruby,

    Please forgive my absence. To my great dismay, I have been called away on business. I very much look forward to seeing you in one week's time and to the resumption of our reading Dickens. Until then, I will think only of you.

My fondest thoughts,
Edwin

Edwin addressed the envelope with Ruby's name and the location of the learning center and sealed the letter inside.

"My coachman will deliver it personally to Miss Spriggs tomorrow morning," Murd promised.

⋎

Ruby knew that Saturday would come, but it was longer in coming than she wished. The week contained the usual number of days with the usual number of hours. If only time might pass more quickly until she was with Edwin, at which time it would please her if time were suspended.

Edwin was not at the learning center when Ruby arrived on Saturday morning.

There was a problem that took her mind off of him for a bit. A large man with a thick dark beard barged in with his wife in tow. Ruby had seen the woman before with her sons at the learning center.

"We have never been readers in our family," the man raged. "It is idleness. It is folly."

"Pay him no heed," his wife said. "He does not mean what he says."

Before the dialogue could unfold further, another man approached.

"Miss Spriggs?"

"Yes?"

"I have a letter for you."

Ruby took the envelope and opened it:

Dear Miss Spriggs,

I am Edwin Chatfield's employer. I wish to speak with you about a matter of supervening importance. My coachman will escort you to my home.

Sincerely,

Alexander Murd

Ruby's heart beat rapidly. She feared that Edwin might be hurt.
She had no inkling—none, I am quite sure—of what lay ahead.

The coachman drove Ruby to Murd's home. Another servant
met her at the door and brought her inside.

Ruby had been in Octavius Joy's home many times, so she was
familiar with elegance. This was wealth of a different order. There
was richness and splendour at every turn. The house was filled
with luxurious things. The most expensive furniture, the softest
carpets, beautiful gilded mirrors, articles of dazzling ornament.

The servant escorted Ruby to Murd's study.

Isabella Murd was sitting in a chair. She stared at Ruby with
cruel eyes and a haughty smile. A man that Ruby presumed to be
Isabella's father sat behind an ornate desk. He gestured for Ruby
to sit. There was a dark expression on his face.

Ruby sat with her hands folded in her lap. She was aware of the
contrast between her plain clothes and the fine attire that the man
and Isabella wore.

The man studied her at his leisure, not speaking for a time.
Ruby's face, he observed, was remarkably pleasant. She was prettier than he had thought she would be.

Ruby grew a bit flush with the awareness that she was under
inspection. But she looked steadily at the man's hard eye.

Finally, he spoke.

"I believe that you have met my daughter, Isabella. I am Edwin's
employer, Alexander Murd."

His manner was cool, and he spoke with the tone of one who
had assumed the high moral ground.

"We meet under troubling circumstances," Murd said. "This is
an awkward and delicate situation, and I request that you honour
me with your full attention. I will be as plain with you as I can
possibly be, so there is no misunderstanding."

Ruby waited.

"Edwin has asked me to inform you that he will no longer be coming to the learning center. He was not there today because he does not wish to see you again. He requested that my daughter and I speak to you instead."

Murd turned toward his daughter.

"Would you make certain that the door is tightly shut. Servants have a way of listening, and I would be uncomfortable if our conversation were overheard."

Isabella followed her father's instruction. Murd returned his attention to Ruby.

"I have heard that you harbour sentiments, fantasies—I do not know what to call them—for Edwin. You are a clever young woman for your station in life. But your attachment for this young man is more fantasy than real. You have been a plaything for Edwin, a trifle for the occupation of an idle hour. When I was a young man, I had a few such toys myself.

"The object of my bringing you here," Murd continued, "is to assure you that there is no more hope for a future between you and Edwin than there would be had he died last night. You could change the colour of the sky from blue to green as easily as you could be with him. Edwin is far above you. You are not worthy of him."

"Edwin is the best judge of that," Ruby said defiantly.

"Hold your tongue when I am speaking to you. The relations between us are unfortunate. But they are of your making, not mine."

"I am the best judge of my own affairs."

"But not of Edwin's."

It was a strange contrast, the two hearts beating opposite one another. The innocent heart of the guileless young woman, palpitating with anxiety and apprehension. And the villainous heart of the cunning man with his wily calculations and plots.

"I will break your spirit," Murd thought. Then he looked at Ruby. It seemed to her as though not a muscle in his face moved except for those he used in speaking.

"I have done some investigation out of concern for Edwin. There is a mystery about your birth. Have you ever wondered about your mother and father? What fantasy were you told?"

He knew not to play too fine a game. He held her now by a thread. If he drew the thread too tight, it might snap.

"Were you ever told of your mother's profession?"

"I did not know that my mother had a profession," Ruby answered. There was uncertainty now in her voice.

"It is in the police files. Your mother is your disgrace, and you were hers. She was a whore."

For the first time, Isabella spoke.

"Ruby is a harlot's name," she all but shrieked. "You may think that your fortune lies between your legs—"

Murd silenced his daughter with the slight raise of his hand.

Ruby had heard enough.

"I have never been in this house before," she said, rising from her chair. "And I will never be here again."

"Sit down," Murd instructed. "You will hear me now, or you will hear me later. But later will be too late for Edwin's well-being. If he suffers, I trust you will remember that I brought you into my home today, and you acted in a manner that brought him harm."

A shadowy veil was dropping round her. Ruby sat. Yet there was still spirit within her, and Murd understood that she would fight him.

He was accustomed to balancing chances and calculating odds in his mind by studying the faces of those who sat opposite him in negotiations. He was able to form conclusions quickly and arrive at cunning deductions. Now was the time to move to the marrow of his persuasion.

"Do you have genuine care for Edwin, or does nothing move you beyond your own selfish longings?"

"I have feelings for Edwin."

Murd signaled with his eyes, and Isabella spoke again: "There is no hope that you will ever call him your own. He is promised to me."

"That is absurd," Ruby scoffed.

"Is it?" Murd asked. Then he handed Ruby a letter.

Dear Mr. Murd,

Thank you for welcoming me into your home and sharing your family and friends so graciously with me. I am most appreciative.

Sincerest wishes,
Edwin

Ruby face coloured and she breathed quickly for a moment. She recognized Edwin's hand from the inscription in the book that he had given to her.

The moment passed.

"What of it?" she said. "Perhaps Edwin was a guest in your home for dinner."

But there was a kernel of doubt in her eyes.

"Then how do you explain this?" Murd asked, his last word sounding like the hiss of a snake.

He handed Ruby a second letter.

Dear Miss Murd,

Thank you for the pleasure of your company this past Saturday evening. You have brought the most beautiful music into my life. I envision a future with laughing children learning to read and write.

Very truly yours,
Edwin

Ruby trembled. Murd saw the movement and knew its value. The hook had been baited and was lodged firmly in the mouth of the fish. All that remained was to skillfully reel the catch in.

"What does this mean?" Ruby asked, staring at the letter.

"You may draw your own conclusions," Murd said.

Now Isabella was speaking.

"You poor deluded girl. Where is your arrogance now? You are a cloth for dirty hands, a piece of pollution picked up from the river to be made game with for an hour before being tossed back to its original place."

Ruby was feeling a bit faint. "Could I have a glass of water, please?"

Isabella's face contorted into something more hateful than before.

"A glass of water. Bring a bucket and throw it over her head."

Murd poured a glass of water from a decanter on his desk and handed it to Ruby. Her face was fully flush now, and he congratulated himself on how well calculated his moves had been in striking at her spirit. The worst that was within him had gained the upper hand. There was something unnatural in the calmness of his voice, spoken while her world was crumbling.

"Marriage is a civil contract," Murd said. "People marry to better their worldly condition. It is an affair of house and furniture, of servants and stables, and the proper breeding of children. Society requires that a young man such as Edwin place himself in a better position by marriage. If Edwin were in a more primitive state, if he lived under a roof of leaves and kept cows and sheep instead of mastering the coal trade, your little fantasy would be less foolish. But Edwin does not live under leaves and keep cows and sheep. He is learning to be a man of business. He is as far removed from your reach as Heaven will be if you continue your wanton conduct."

Ruby sat silent, weighing the letters that had been written in Edwin's hand and the fact of his absence from the learning center. Helplessness and desolation welled up in her breast like blood from an inward wound.

Isabella was speaking again.

"When Edwin and I are married, we will have a large house in a fashionable neighborhood, a footman to open the door, a housemaid, a cook, a butler to wait at our table, and a carriage and horses to drive about in. I believe that is more than the dowry you would be able to offer him."

"But we still have a problem," Murd said, fixing his eyes on Ruby. "The whispers about your attentions to Edwin have begun. It is not town talk yet. It is not yet cried in the streets or chalked upon the walls. But whispers have been heard. Perhaps you are unversed in the realities of civilized life. And so, recognizing the truths of the world we live in, I feel compelled to remind you of the immense disadvantage at which you have placed Edwin. His future promises all of the honour and wealth that a man of his talent can attain. But his future will be bleak if he is seen as mingling with a woman such as yourself, who has fastened herself as a leech upon his progress in the world.

"You are a dark cloud that is shadowing Edwin's future. If the situation is not corrected immediately, I will have no choice but to dismiss him from his employment. Not only will Edwin lose his job, he will be disgraced. It will ruin his career irretrievably. Therefore, you shall pledge never to see Edwin again. You will abandon all pretense that he has feeling for you and forget him as the object of your desire. You will relinquish any and all ties to the relationship. Is that clear?"

There was no response.

"What are your thoughts?" Murd pressed.

"I think that you are a horrible man."

"I am not interested in what you think of me. I am interested in what you think of ruining Edwin. Those good looks of yours are worth money, and you shall make money off of them. But not at the expense of my reputation and my family. Either we will come to a friendly agreement today or we will come to an unfriendly explosion. If it is the former, Edwin will not be hurt. If it is the latter, I have told you what will happen."

"When would you dismiss him?"

"Perhaps tomorrow. And one thing more. The law intervenes to prevent good English citizens from being troubled by unlawful intrusions upon their daily life. Properly implemented, it takes hold of a transgressor and punishes him, or her as the case may be. I regret the need to be impolite. But if you are ever seen with Edwin again, I will give you over to the police."

It was too much. The colours of Ruby's life were changing.

"You claim to have high regard for Edwin," Murd said in a calm measured voice. "If that is so, I am sure that it would be a source of great unhappiness to you were you the cause of ruining his future."

"She cares nothing for Edwin," Isabella interposed. "She cares for no one but herself."

A look from Murd silenced his daughter.

He returned his attention to Ruby.

"And one thing more is required of you," he said in a calm measured voice. "You have compelled us to this course. The fault is yours, not ours. If Edwin is to be saved from ruin, it will not be enough that you abandon your foolish designs on him. You must remove yourself from London."

"I do not understand your words."

"Then I will speak more clearly. You will leave London tomorrow."

"London is my home."

"You will be provided with travel and funds to begin a new life. You will put an ocean between yourself and Edwin. It will not break his heart to lose you, nor would it have broken his heart had you never been found. Your departure will be a relief to him. He has told me so. There is no other way to mitigate the harm that you have done."

Ruby's thoughts were colliding now in a chaotic jumble.

"I understand, now, Isabella's hatred of me . . . If I do as Murd says, Edwin will maintain his position and hope. If I do not, Edwin will be plunged into ruin . . . I am shamed by my past . . . In London, I will cause suffering and sorrow . . . I cannot reason clearly . . . I am humiliated for thinking that Edwin might love me . . . I have seen the words written in Edwin's own hand. He dreams of a future with Isabella and their laughing happy children . . . I do not want to believe it. I have no choice but to believe it . . . I cannot live with this."

"Take warning by what I have said," Murd intoned. "What I say, I mean. And what I threaten, I will do."

Isabella picked the second of Edwin's two letters off of her father's desk and waved it before her face like a fan.

Ruby was broken.

"Where would you have me go?" she asked quietly.

"To America."

Murd had borne his part in the proceeding with a cold passionless demeanor. There was no change now.

"I will arrange for a carriage to meet you at your residence tomorrow morning at six o'clock. Before boarding the ship, you will be given a pouch with coins that are negotiable in America. If you do not board the ship, Edwin will lose everything that he has worked for his entire life and I will take further action against you."

Ruby sat silent with her head down.

"I should like assurance of your acquiescence to these terms."

"You may feel assured."

"It is all arranged then," Murd said, allowing a touch of cheerfulness to creep into his voice.

"I wish to see Edwin."

"I do not understand your request."

"It is plain enough. I wish to see Edwin before I leave England."

"I have made it plain; he does not wish to see you."

"He must know what I feel for him."

The fish had been in its dying throes. Murd feared now that the line might snap.

"What you feel for Edwin is of no consequence. The nub of the matter is what he does not feel for you."

"I will not leave London without first speaking with Edwin."

"I will make an arrangement with you," Murd said, thinking as he spoke. "Edwin knows of our meeting today. Given the embarrassing circumstances of the moment, he and I, both of us, would prefer that no one else know. Give me your pledge of silence with regard to all that has happened, and I will deliver a letter from you to Edwin. That way, your feelings will be known to him."

Murd handed Ruby a piece of paper and an ornate fountain pen. There was a glass inkwell with silver trim on his desk. She dipped the pen in the ink and began to write:

My Dearest Edwin,

I am sorry for the discomfort that I have caused you. I hoped that you might love me someday as I love you. But I understand now that my foolishness has threatened your happiness and your future.

If I did wrong—and I may have done much—it was out of love and because of my want of wisdom.

Think of me at my best.
Ruby

When she was done, she put down the pen and turned her face away so the paper that was to be her messenger would not bear her tears.

"I will give this to Edwin," Murd promised. "Now let us review your instructions. To spare everyone from shame, you will tell no one about what has happened. You will leave London tomorrow. My coachman will confirm to me that you are on board the ship to America. I expect you to act with honour. Do I have your word that you will adhere to the terms of our agreement?"

"I will keep my word."

"Very well, then. There will be a few tears, perhaps. But soon, I am sure, you will be happy. Class and rank are of less consideration in America than here in England. Someday, you will have a good husband and children."

Murd rang a bell on his desk. A servant appeared at the door.

"Kindly escort Miss Spriggs from the house."

"Yes, sir."

"And watch her carefully," Isabella instructed. "Make certain that she does not take anything that belongs to us on her way out."

Ruby stared Isabella in the eye.

"I take away no hope, Miss Murd. But if you ask me whether I love Edwin, I will tell you that I do."

After Ruby left, Iabella's face bore a triumphant look. She was pleased with the result. It was everything that she had hoped for.

"There are deep wounds in her heart," Murd said.

"I know," Isabella told her father. "I saw it bleeding." There was a cruel smile on her face. "If Edwin touched her with his lips, let it poison her."

Leaning back in his chair, Murd took the letter that Ruby had written for Edwin, opened it, and read it through. "Very nicely worded," he mused. "Full of what people call love, tenderness, and that sort of thing."

He handed the letter to Isabella.

"Do with it what you will," Murd told his daughter.

Isabella laughed a wicked laugh. "It shall be burned."

If the childless kings and queens in fairy tales had known children like Isabella, they would never have asked the fairies to give them young ones.

As for Ruby . . . Her heart beat rapidly as Murd's servant showed her to the door. Her upper front teeth had cut marks into her lower lip. Her face burned as though it were on fire with embarrassment and humiliation. Alexander Murd and his daughter had taken the purity of Ruby's young heart and converted her love for Edwin into an instrument of torture. Having been brought up in a cocoon of love, being not quite eighteen years old, she did not recognize the web of treachery and lies that had been woven round her.

Once she was on the street, Ruby shed bitter tears. The withered dream, the vision of a life with Edwin that she had cherished, lay crushed in her breast. Her heart was broken. Had she known more of the world, she would have done more to question the truth of Murd's words and the meaning of Edwin's letters. But when a young woman is in love, reason sometimes deserts her.

As a child living on the streets, Ruby had been too young to feel shame or know that there was a better world from which she was barred. Now she felt and knew.

"I have made a fool of myself."

Could Edwin have played with her affections in such a cruel manner? Her heart said no. But Edwin had not been at the learning center that morning. Murd's coachman had been sent instead to summon her to Murd's home. Edwin had told Murd where to find her. And he had told Murd that he did not wish to see her again.

Ruby had no more power to rid herself of these thoughts than if they were a stone giant rooted in the ground. It was clear now why Isabella hated her. The reason for Isabella's hatred was written in Edwin's hand.

Ruby's love for Edwin had been a dream. And dreams end with waking. It was not that Edwin's love for her had ceased to be. It had never existed. "What a mad woman I should seem to be if the incredible feelings that I have for him were made plain to others," she thought.

She understood now why Christopher had spoken little to her about her mother. That further tarnished her origins.

Her heart was crushed.

Marie saw the distress in Ruby's face the moment that Ruby returned home to the bakery.

"I must leave," Ruby told her in a voice choked with emotion. "I cannot tell you why, only that I will be safe and that I believe it is God's plan. I know in my heart that it is the right thing to do. You must trust me. I will always love you."

She would tell Marie no more.

"I will write to you as soon as possible. Please ask no questions. It is hard enough for me to leave without saying more."

"Whatever the problem, dear Ruby, tell me what has happened and I will help you."

"It is not possible for you to help."

Marie began to cry.

"Please, do not grieve. It is my duty to go. For many years, I have lived with gratitude and devotion in this home. With Heaven as my witness, wherever I go, my love for you will be unimpaired. It is my witness, too, that I am impelled to travel this road. Nothing can turn me from it."

"I will bring Antonio. Whatever ill fortune has befallen you, he will help us to deal with it."

"Please do not bring Antonio. I beg of you."

"I must."

Ruby's voice rose.

"You cannot. It would only make this moment more painful."

As evening approached, Ruby went to where she kept her belongings, selected the clothes and other possessions she would bring with her, and put them in two large carry bags. If tears were charms that could safeguard a young woman from sorrow, she would have been happy that night. As it were, she wept like a child.

When the bags were packed, Ruby lay down on the bed that had been a comfort to her for so many years. It was an uneasy bed now.

The night was darker than she had ever known. The sounds of London were hushed, save for the bells in church towers.

The bells sounded twice. An hour later, three times. There were other listeners, no doubt, who were glad to hear them. For some, the bells spoke of life and the optimism of another day. For Ruby, the clang of every iron bell was laden with despair.

Then came a distant glimmer in the sky. The death of night, not the birth of morning. The stars grew pale. The feeble light grew stronger.

Ruby rose from her bed. She had not slept. Perhaps Edwin had been told of her departure and would intercede on her behalf. On that slight and fragile thread, her hope for the future depended.

She dressed for the journey and looked out the window. A carriage stood at the curb.

The hour of dreadful separation had come.

Ruby took a last look round the home that she had loved since the early years of childhood. The little room where she had slept peacefully and dreamed such pleasant dreams. The fireplace, where she had warmed herself while sitting on a stool and learning her lessons with Christopher at her side.

There was a foreboding in her heart that she might never see this place again.

At parting, she embraced Marie at the door.

Marie was crying.

"Don't weep, dear Marie. I go away for my own good. Heaven above us knows that it is so."

"You are my child."

"I will be safe. Tell Antonio that I have never held him half so dear as I love him now. And dear Mr. Joy. Tell him that he will be in my heart wherever I go. And know always, dear Marie, that I love you. I have never felt the want of a mother because of your goodness and love."

Ruby held Marie tight in one last embrace.

"And please, tell those I love that I took my leave calm and happy. I promise that I will write to you. Give me your blessing to take with me."

"May angels keep you safe and shower blessings upon your head."

"You will always have my love."

Murd's coachman and a second man stood by the carriage. Ruby stepped outside the bakery and touched her fingers to the door—insensible old wood and iron that it was—then pressed her hand against it.

The man accompanying Murd's coachman took Ruby's bags and put them on the roof of the coach beside a large box that was already there.

The street was quiet. The morning that broke upon Ruby's sight did nothing to lessen the depression that she felt. A drizzling rain came slowly down as though it lacked the spirit to pour. The sky was dark and gloomy. A few early churchgoers moved slowly along. Occasionally, the heavy outline of a hackney coach drew nearer through the mist, rolled by, and was lost again in the fog.

As the carriage rode through the streets of London, reason struggled with fantasy in Ruby's head. She looked out of the window, hoping to see some monstrous phenomenon, perhaps a dragon from her childhood running wild, that would change the plan of her departure.

Everything was too real.

"I will keep my word as I pledged it," Ruby told herself.

She could not bear the thought of perhaps crossing paths with Edwin on the street someday and seeing him with Isabella.

The carriage came to a halt outside of Euston Railway Station.

"I thought I was going to America," Ruby told Murd's coachman.

"The ship leaves from Liverpool," he said.

Only the second man in the carriage would accompany her further.

"My name is Charles," he told Ruby.

Charles waved to a porter, who carried Ruby's bags and the box that had been on top of the carriage to the train. The box, he explained to her, contained provisions for the journey at sea.

They boarded the train and took seats. Twenty minutes later, there was steam, a hiss, a bell, and the train began to move, its wheels clanking and rattling as it left Euston Station.

The building of the railroad was in progress, leaving giant scars across the land. Enormous heaps of earth had been thrown up. Deep trenches cut into the ground. The train travelled through the onrushing landscape, a monster piercing the heart of the countryside with a shriek and roar, belching smoke as it moved through towns. Buildings along the tracks had been undermined and were propped up by great wood beams. Other houses had been knocked down. There were unfinished arches, a chaos of scaffolding.

Ruby was frightened by the ugliness of it all. Was this part of Edwin's world?

She fell asleep several times, but never for more than an hour. There were two connecting carriage rides and two more trains. She cried often, feeling better after she had but not by much.

Several times when the train stopped or the carriage changed horses, Ruby thought of returning to London. More than once, while occupied with these thoughts, she imagined a resemblance to Edwin in men who were walking nearby. Her heart would beat fast. But they were not Edwin.

She travelled on. Night came. Ruby was exhausted when she and Charles arrived in Liverpool early the following morning.

Murd had instructed his man to keep Ruby within his sight at all times until she was on the ship. Charles was there to ensure her departure more than to assist her.

At the docks, smoke poured from the huge red funnel of a great ship, giving promise of serious intentions. Ruby and Charles threaded their way through the noise and bustle. One party of men was carrying fresh provisions to fill the icehouses on the ship. Others were coiling ropes. There seemed to be nothing going on anywhere or in any mind other than preparation for the voyage.

Ruby realized that she did not know where in America she was going.

"To Boston," Charles told her.

Porters looking like so many Atlases were carrying the luggage of the wealthier-looking passengers. Charles engaged the services of one to carry Ruby's load. He made no more of her box and bags than an elephant would have made of a maharaja on its back. He lifted Ruby's belongings and moved along as if he could go faster with them than without.

Charles followed her every step of the way. He presented Ruby's ticket at a gate, and she was directed to an area where a mass of poorly dressed men and women with children and boxes and bags were standing.

"I leave you now," Charles said. "Do not forget these."

He handed Ruby a pouch with gold coins.

"These will have value in America. I believe that they were promised to you."

A signal was given, and the mob moved forward. Ruby showed her ticket. Her name was compared to those on a registry. She was given a number—"27"—and instructed to move with the others.

Dozens of seamen—well-muscled men, browned and hardened by their exposure to weather—were in view.

"All guns, gunpowder, knives, and other weapons must be turned over to the captain," one of the seaman called out again and again. "They will be returned to you upon disembarking in America."

Ruby struggled with her bags and box.

"We're going across," one of the seamen said, as if the ship were a ferry crossing the Thames.

On board the ship, Ruby was directed down a ladder and shown to a bunk—"27"—not much larger than her bed at home had been. It was to be shared with a mother and two young children. People swarmed around her, stumbling over each other amidst confusion.

This was steerage, the lowest deck and cheapest class of ticket on the ship. Ruby had not known of cabins and steerage before.

A bell sounded. Ruby returned with some of the others to the main deck. Small boats pulled the vessel away from the dock. Like a giant receiving the breath of life, the huge ship throbbed and its great wheels turned. Gathering speed, it moved away from the harbour.

The shoreline of England grew more distant. Ruby stared longingly at it until her tear-filled eyes were as sore as her heart. The desolate feeling within her deepened and widened. Soon, much too soon, there was nothing to be seen but water.

She felt now the full weight of the change upon her life and all that she had lost. Love, family, friendship, and home were shattered.

"Where am I going? What have I done?"

She wished that she could tell the crew to stop the ship, turn it around, and return to England. All that she had known and loved was gone.

Her destiny lay in an unknown land far beyond the horizon.

Book 3

CHAPTER 7

Edwin's train left Euston Railway Station at eleven o'clock on Friday morning. For most of the day, it rolled through the English countryside, booming into the darkness of a tunnel now and then before bursting out into sunny meadows and fields where sheep were grazing.

There were several stops in cities and another train that rumbled through woods, across a river where a mill was turning, down into the earth again, and up once more into the sunshine where villages clustered and church steeples rose.

All the while, Edwin thought of Ruby.

"She has made a change within me. It was such a grand sensation when she put her arm through mine. More than anything, I would like that feeling again."

As the train neared its final stop, the landscape grew coarse. Mounds of brambles and weeds were heaped together. In the distance, a town lay shrouded in a dark haze. At least, Edwin surmised the existence of a town because of the sullen blotch upon the horizon.

The train advanced closer to the dismal sight. Stagnant pools where nothing green could live sweltered by the rails. Coal dust darkened shrunken leaves. There was little grass, nor had any bud fulfilled its promise. A great amount of iron lay about, twisted into various shapes. Axles, wedges, cogs, wheels, cranks, all rusting with age. Then huge whirling machines, spinning and writhing like tortured creatures, clanking their iron chains and screeching as though in torment.

The train came to a halt in the shadow of a large brick building. A gloomy spirit fell upon Edwin. Dark smoke poured out of tall chimneys on every side, fouling the air and obscuring the setting sun with a dense black cloud.

※

Man has extracted materials from the earth since the beginning of civilization. The earliest of these were used to make tools and weapons. The ancient Egyptians mined turquoise, copper, and gold for ornamentation. Succeeding empires advanced the means of securing whatever of value lay beneath the surface.

Colliery, or coal mining as it is also known, is as old as history. Early man gathered coal for fire. The Romans and Chinese used coal before Christ was born.

Prior to the 1800s, coal was mined in large measure from visible outcrops or deposits close to the surface of the earth. Pits shaped like upside down bells were carved into the ground with no roof support of any kind. These bell pits were as much as two hundred fifty feet deep. When one collapsed, it opened the surrounding terrain for more mining.

In the second half of the eighteenth century, a revolution in industrial processes led to an increase in the use of steam power and an exponential increase in the demand for coal. At the same time, shaft mining became the most common form of mining in England. Miners learned to use timber to support shaft walls and the roofs of tunnels, which enabled them to dig deeper into the earth and burrow further away from the shaft. Then steam pumps became more sophisticated in removing water that seeped into tunnels, allowing shafts to extend even further into the ground.

By 1850, more than two hundred thousand English men, women, and children laboured in mines.

Colliery has made some people rich. It has cost many more their lives. A shaft is dug into the ground, often a quarter of a mile deep. Tunnels supported by timber brattice extend a hundred yards or more away from the shaft. The pits are mined round the clock by workers, who labour in shifts as long as twelve hours. They see as much of the sun as a man might hope for were he placed in a coffin.

A man's life is measured in years. For coal miners, each birthday warns of passing another marker that stands between them and the grave. The boys have a feeling of immortality. They view going into the mines as a rite of passage to becoming a man. By the time they are old enough to understand fully what is involved, they are locked into their mean existence.

The mine tunnels are places of slow torture, dark narrow ovens filled with black soot in summer and clammy cold in winter. The miners crawl upon hands and knees, their bodies touching the roof and walls.

Rats are everywhere.

The shadow of death is omnipresent. Most of the men die prematurely from diseases of the lungs and heart or lose the strength that they rely upon for their livelihood as a consequence of the debilitating wear and tear that their bodies endure.

The noise of digging and blasting is constant in their claustrophobic underground world. More ominous are the everyday warning sounds of strata shifting, rocks falling, roof timber cracking, and water dripping. A miner grows accustomed to these sounds or is broken by them.

Rock falls from collapsing tunnels and the rush of water if an underground stream breaches a tunnel wall are ever present threats. Poisonous and flammable gasses accumulate in air pockets within coal deposits. If one of these foul pockets is penetrated, the release of gas can lead to death by suffocation.

The miners carry Davy lamps in the tunnels. The flame is encased beneath an iron gauze top knit tightly enough to prevent it from passing through the mesh. If the flame in a Davy lamp enlarges or turns blue, it is a danger signal that gas is in the air.

But the light that the Davy lamps emit is poor. The men can make more money by working with a full light than they can with the gauze tops fastened on. Sometimes they open their lamps underground. If gas is present, the result can be a catastrophic explosion.

Not a week passes without men dying in English mines. Women and children too.

In 1838, a stream overflowed into a mine shaft after a violent thunderstorm in Silkstone in northern England. Fifteen boys between the ages of nine and twelve and eleven girls between the ages of eight and sixteen were killed. In the aftermath of the disaster, Queen Victoria ordered an inquiry. A royal commission headed by Lord Anthony Ashley was formed. Lord Ashley's study broadened into an investigation of overall conditions in the mines. His final report led to the passage by Parliament of the Mines Act of 1842, which prohibits boys under the age of ten and all women from working underground in mines. Five years later, the Ten Hours Bill, which limits the length of time that women and children can work to ten hours a day, was enacted into law.

There are four inspectors in all of England charged with enforcing the Mines Act. It is largely ignored.

❦

Julian White, who oversaw Murd's mining operations in Lancashire, was at the station to meet Edwin when the train arrived. He was a well-fed man of medium height, about forty years of age with a ruddy complexion and thinning hair.

"I have instructions from Mr. Murd to show you a bit of the business," White said as he escorted Edwin to an inn nearby. "You will be in Lancashire until Wednesday. Make yourself comfortable tonight. I will come for you at seven o'clock tomorrow morning."

The inn that Edwin was lodged in had seen better days. He ordered chicken for dinner. The bird's tendons and ligaments extended into its breast as a gnarled tree might strike roots into the earth. Its thighs were hard enough to warrant the conclusion that the bird had spent the better part of its life in rigorous exercise.

Julian White returned on Saturday morning and walked with Edwin to the mine site. There, Edwin was introduced to the overseer, a man named Jonathan Hunt.

Hunt had the responsibility of giving the miners their work orders each day. He was hard-featured and stocky with the stubble of a coarse beard on his chin. Hunt talked as he, White, and Edwin walked.

"The pit here is about eleven hundred feet deep. At present, we are mining a seam of coal that extends westward from the shaft at an average of five feet thick."

The young men at work at the mine site looked strong and able. The older men seemed worn out. A heavy burden was written on their faces, and their bodies were bent as if by the weight of a great trouble. The women were pale and weary. The children had no childhood in their eyes.

"The hewers work with picks below the surface," Hunt explained, continuing Edwin's education. "The miners who push the wagons underground are called putters. Hurriers pull the wagons. Each tunnel is divided into sections by canvas flaps that are lifted and lowered to regulate the flow of air. The men who lift and lower the flaps are called trappers."

"It is a dangerous business," the overseer added. "Live and you learn. Nearly die, and you learn quicker."

The following day, Sunday, was a day of rest in the mines. Edwin thought of going to church, but decided that he could commune with the Almighty just as well while walking about the town.

The inn was on a dismal street. A gaunt tree with a blackened trunk and leaves that rattled rather than rustled when a breeze filtered through them stood outside the door. Farther down the street, a long row of mean houses with windows patched with paper told of the poverty there.

The air was tainted and offensive. The entire town seemed unhealthy for want of clean air. Edwin could only wonder what the air in the mines was like. There was coal dust on everything. It was May, but not a single flower was in sight.

"Today, I was to have spent the entire day with Ruby," Edwin ruefully thought.

He imagined Ruby receiving his letter at the learning center the previous morning.

"She knows the reason for my absence and understands my eagerness to see her again."

Monday morning, by prearrangement, Edwin went to Julian White's office. There were two rooms and a staff consisting of a clerk and secretary, each polite but not particularly friendly.

When Edwin was at the mine site on Saturday, he had felt out of place with his London clothes. He arrived at White's office without a jacket and neckwear.

White talked a bit about how coal was transported from the Lancashire mine to various parts of England. Then Edwin expressed the desire to revisit the mine site and speak with some of the miners.

White seemed reluctant to pursue it.

"Mr. Murd tells me that you have a way with people. But too much familiarity breeds disrespect for authority."

Edwin repeated his request, suggesting that he would go alone if White chose not to go with him. Faced with that alternative, White agreed to accompany him on the visit.

At the mine site, Edwin watched as coal was pulled up the shaft in large open containers to the mouth of the pit. The dust in the air was a thick constant presence. At five o'clock, there was a change in shifts. Hundreds of men came out of the earth. More than a few women and children rose from the underground with them.

One of the men made eye contact with Edwin, perhaps wondering who this young man was. His face was horribly scarred.

White reached out a hand as if to gently restrain Edwin.

Edwin ignored him.

"What happened?" he asked the miner.

"Six months ago, some rocks fell. I could not see what was in front of me, so I lifted the top off my lamp. And pheuww! There was an explosion. I was lucky," the man continued. "There was not much gas, just a small pocket. It scorched my face, and the skin peeled off. These things happen. I have been careless many times. All of us are."

As the man spoke, a young woman—more likely, a girl—stood by his side. Her torn, coarse dirty clothes bore the marks of work in the pit.

"How old are you?" Edwin asked.

"Fourteen, sir."

"She is my daughter," the man with the scarred face said.

"How long were you underground today?"

"Ten hours," the girl answered.

"What do you do down there?"

"I hurry the corfs."

A voice from behind sounded.

"And she has not seen the sun high in the sky except on a Sunday for almost a year."

Edwin turned.

The speaker was a large round-shouldered man about thirty years of age with a good deal of hair and whisker. Most likely, its natural colour was red, but coal dust and smoke made it darker.

"You asked what this young woman does in the pit," the man said, looking directly at Edwin. "So I will tell you. A thick girdle is bound round her waist. A chain is passed between her legs, with one end of the chain attached to the girdle and the other end to a corf filled with coal. She then crawls on all fours as the chain passes between what might be called her hind legs, and she pulls the corf through tunnels as narrow as a sewer. She is clothed now, so you cannot see the price she pays. The girdle blisters her sides. Her skin breaks and blood runs down her body. Her legs are swollen. A more indecent sight cannot be found in a brothel."

"That is quite enough," Julian White interrupted.

"And her older brother died in the mines," the man continued, oblivious to the warning. "Although older seems a strange word, since he was ten years old at the time."

"You are overstepping propriety," White snapped. "Another word and your employment will terminate."

"Begging your pardon, sir," the man said with more than a trace of mockery.

"Be gone."

"As you wish, sir."

Neither White nor Edwin spoke in the wake of the man's departure.

Edwin broke the silence.

"I have a question, sir."

"What is it?"

"My understanding is that the law forbids all women from working underground in mines."

A look similar to the look that Edwin had seen many times on Alexander Murd's face crossed White's eyes.

"I object on principle to government interference in the management of any private business."

"Why is that, sir?"

"Mining is a complex science that does not lend itself to oversight by those who are unfamiliar with the trade."

At the end of the day, Edwin returned to the inn. He was readying to go to the common room for dinner when there was a knock on his door.

"It is Ethan Crowl," a voice said. There was a pause. "You do not know my name. But if you open the door, you will know my face."

Edwin opened the door. The miner who had confronted him at the pit regarding the conditions under which the fourteen-year-old girl laboured stood before him.

The two men eyed each other.

"How did you know where to find me?"

"There is only one inn in town," Crowl answered. "And the housekeeping staff is not always discreet."

"Why have you sought me out?"

"I trust your face."

Edwin extended his hand.

"My name is Edwin Chatfield."

Crowl's handshake was firm. "I would like to tell you more about the mines," he said.

Edwin offered his visitor the only chair in the room and sat on the bed.

"When society sees a labourer who speaks out," Crowl began, "it warns, 'He is suspicious. Watch that fellow.' The men who own the mines look upon us as toys to be played with for their advantage and discarded when broken. They see us in no other light. It is harder than you think to grow up right in a place like this. Pay us a fair wage so our children can have decent homes, so we can have better food when we are working. Treat us with fairness, and we will be as grateful as men can be. As things now stand, the extraction of coal from the ground costs less than the transportation of that coal to market."

"I have no control over what you and the others are paid."

"I know that," Crowl said. "I am here simply to tell you of our lives. I saw you at the pit on Saturday and again today. You looked at us as men and women, not as beasts of burden. It was in your eyes. You studied everything you saw. When you leave this place, I want you to remember what is here. Someday, perhaps, you will be able to help us."

"What more should I know?"

"Each of us has a story. I will tell you mine. When a vein of coal is exhausted, it is the practice to make a new cutting that extends off the tunnel until another vein is found. Six years ago, two dozen men and I were cutting from an exhausted vein. We holed into a tunnel that had been worked years before and was filled with water. Some of the water came in on us. We moved to the shaft and were hoisted to the surface. Then we were told that there was no danger and we should go back underground.

"We did as we were told. Two hours later, the roof of the tunnel collapsed and water rushed in. Seven were drowned. The rest of us moved to the highest part of the air course and huddled together with little air to breathe and no way of escape. Death was staring us in the face. To add to the horror, because of the fear of gas, our lamps were put out. We were in total darkness. One of the men, twenty-two years old, shrieked in agony. He cried out the names of his wife and infant son again and again, and tore his hair from his head. He died two hours later. Some of us sat silent, awaiting death's arrival. Others prayed aloud or wept.

"My own mind was not right. I was dazed. A rock had fallen on my head. To keep me out of the mud and water, a young man named Adam Lockett took me in his arms and laid me across his lap. I went to sleep. When I awoke, he was dead. We were tempted to drink some of the water in the tunnel, but it was sulfuric. To drink meant certain death. We were in this condition for two days and two nights. During this time, four more men died.

"On the third day, help arrived. The first person to break through was my brother, Joseph. The first man he reached was Robert Watts. Joseph asked, 'Is Ethan alive?' 'He is,' Robert told him. My brother crawled over bodies until he got to me. He shook me and called me by name, and I answered. Then he took me in his arms and, as the water had risen to within a foot of the tunnel roof, Joseph lay on his back and paddled himself through the tunnel, holding me above the water until we reached the shaft. These things happen all the time. And the business of mining goes on the same, with no change in the practices that lead to disaster."

Edwin sat silent.

"What about the coroners' inquests?" he asked at last. "The law of England requires them so that the cause of an untimely death is addressed."

Crowl laughed a bitter laugh.

"The coroners are placed in their office by mining interests. After each fatality, a lawyer for the mining company shapes their findings. Sometimes the coroner puts his name to the report while the inquest is still pending."

"Is it always that way?"

"The inquest reports are in the courthouse. Look at them and judge for yourself."

It had been planned that Edwin would spend Tuesday at Julian White's office before returning to London the following day. Instead, he went to the courthouse.

The building, like most of the substantial buildings in the town, was made of brick. Its windows were so encrusted with dirt that the bright May sunshine seemed dim. Edwin stated his reason for coming to a clerk and was directed to a room where the coroners' inquest reports were kept.

The law of England provides that no man, woman, or child who has come to a violent end shall be buried without a judicial investigation into the cause of death. This is done to determine whether any individual, by neglect or criminal intent, was responsible for the death and should be held accountable. The inquests are also conducted with an eye toward learning from the fatality and, as far as humanly possible, preventing similar calamities from happening again.

But eagle flights of the law are rare. More commonly, the legal process is marked by slippery crawlings. Writs are issued, judgments are signed, various machinations are put in play largely for the enrichment of the ruling class.

The facts of each coroner's inquest report that Edwin studied differed. But the conclusion was always the same.

An explosion resulted in a fire and the death of six men as well as four boys ranging in age from nine to twelve. One of the miners had been using a naked lamp to work more quickly while blasting was under way.

Nine miners were being hoisted up a shaft when a badly rusted chain broke. They plummeted eight hundred feet to their death.

Two men were suffocated by poisonous gas, having been instructed to remain in the tunnel after a leak of noxious air was suspected. Their bodies were recovered three months later, by which time they had been reduced to skeletons.

In each instance, the inquest report concluded, "Accidental Death Without Blame."

At noon, Edwin made his way to Julian White's office.

"Is it possible that the company could do more to protect the men and women who work in the mines?" he asked.

"These matters are investigated fully," White responded. "The coroner conducts a thorough investigation. In every instance, the facts have been clear that there was no wrongdoing on the company's part. If you think logically for a moment, you will come to the conclusion that it is in the company's best interests to prevent accidents from happening inasmuch as they interfere with the profitable operation of the mines."

"What causes the accidents to happen?"

White shrugged.

"It is in the nature of mining that these things occur, just as it is natural that some men are lost at sea. Jonathan Hunt is employed at a generous salary to examine the pits and ensure that they are safe."

"How is that done?"

"You are here for me to teach you about the business of mining. You are not here for me to instruct you on how to become a miner."

"I would like to revisit the mine," Edwin said.

"I advise against it. There has been a hint of rebellion among the men as of late."

"With all due respect, sir, I wish to go."

"Then you will go alone. I cannot vouch for your safety."

Ethan Crowl was not in sight when Edwin arrived at the mine. Edwin asked several of the men if they knew where he was without satisfaction. Then a man with a stooped gait approached. His face was worn by time and notable for a deep gash, now healed into an ugly seam, that must have laid his cheekbone bare when inflicted.

"He is in the pit," the man said. "Wait here. He will be up in an hour."

Two hours passed before Crowl appeared. Edwin discussed the coroner's inquest findings with him.

"Why do the men work without tops on their lamps?" Edwin asked.

"If the colliers do not mine a given amount of coal each week, they are fined a certain sum per basket. No abatement is made if they have been required to curtail or leave their work because of safety concerns. Every man should be compelled to work with the top on his lamp, and his wages should be raised so that he may earn, under that disadvantage, as much as he is paid now. If that step were taken, far fewer lives would be lost from explosion. But that would lower the company's profit."

Crowl looked directly into Edwin's eyes.

"Mining will never be safe. But it can be made less dangerous. The present conditions exist because men like Alexander Murd have persuaded the ruling class that it is inevitable and thus acceptable that miners will suffocate, drown, and burn to death by the thousands each year. One wonders how Murd can lay his head upon a pillow in peace at night."

"I would like to go into the mine," Edwin said.

The words seemed spoken impetuously, but they were not. Edwin had been thinking about them for three days.

"Are you certain?" Crowl pressed.

"I am."

"It is not a game."

"I understand."

"Very well then."

Men who are about to descend into a mine shaft climb into what is known as a bucket. The bucket is then lowered with the aid of a windlass, a piece of heavy machinery that consists of a horizontal barrel rotated by the turn of a crank with a chain wound round the barrel. The less sophisticated windlasses are powered by a horse that is harnessed to a wheel and walks in a circle, clockwise or counterclockwise as the case may be, to lift and lower the bucket. This windlass was powered by an engine.

"I will go down with you," Crowl said.

Two other miners joined them. One was a strongly built young man with a handsome face. The other was about forty years old with a weary expression that had worn into his features as hard weather wears into rock.

The bucket descended into the shaft.

Deeper and deeper.

The light of the sun grew dimmer until everything was dark.

Edwin's heart was pounding. His survival was now linked to a handful of men above and below the surface of the earth. And to fate.

The air in the shaft grew more fetid and humid.

The bucket hit bottom at eleven hundred feet.

The darkness was claustrophobic.

Crowl lit his lamp, keeping the top on.

Edwin saw an opening in the shaft wall, a tunnel four feet high. No sunlight had ever made its way inside.

Crowl nodded toward the tunnel.

"After you, Mr. Chatfield."

The tunnel had a forbidding look and an earthy deadly smell.

"I would prefer to not go in the tunnel," Edwin said.

"Why not?"

"I am afraid."

"Of a hole in the ground?"

"I know that you do this on most days of your life, but I do not wish to endure it."

Crowl reached an arm around Edwin's shoulders.

"You are braver than you think you are, my friend from London. The pit is more cruel than battle."

Crowl gave a signal, and the bucket began an ascent toward the top of the shaft.

There was palpable relief on Edwin's face when they reached the surface.

"I like you," Crowl said.

"The feeling is mutual. You bear your wrongs more nobly than I could bear them were they mine."

While travelling back to London on Wednesday, Edwin considered all that he had seen. He had long been aware of suffering among the poor. But he was shaken by his ignorance regarding the mines.

The miners were slaves of a grinding iron-handed system. Day after day, they toiled underground in crowded spaces, breathing noxious air. Dark tunnels that might collapse upon them at any moment formed the narrow boundary of their existence. They worked in these wretched places. And died in them.

Edwin thought now of the children that he had seen on the streets the past few days. These children were unfamiliar with such fables as the golden innocence of youth, the prime of life, and a hale old age. They had no future other than demeaning servitude to the conditions of the day.

Alexander Murd was a man of business. He dealt in contracts, bank notes, and cheques. The coal never touched his hands. But that coal, on land that he owned, was the stuff of which a vast fortune had been made.

The miners were under Murd's control. Every legal right, power, and influence was on his side. He grew richer every day by exploiting their harsh never-ending labour.

Edwin chastised himself for his naïveté in believing in Murd and for his past ignorance regarding the mines. For much of the journey home, he wrestled with the moral implications inherent in working for Murd and also with the practical considerations relating to his well-paying employment.

He thought often of Ruby, as he had for most of the time that he had been in Lancashire.

"She came into my life like the glimpse of a better world. Saturday, when I see her again, cannot come too soon."

The first thing that Edwin did upon arriving at his chambers in London was take a long bath to rid himself of the slimy witch ointment that the air in Lancashire had deposited upon him. The following morning, he returned to the office.

Shortly before noon, Arthur Abbott told Edwin that Mr. Murd wished to speak with him.

Murd was seated at his desk when Edwin entered his private room. An account book with numbers arranged in precisely drawn columns lay open before him.

"I trust that your visit to Lancashire was enlightening," Murd said, looking up from the ledger.

"Yes, sir."

"I received a report from Julian White by courier earlier this morning. Mr. White informs me that you spent a considerable amount of time in Lancashire fraternizing with the miners."

"I spent some time with them, sir."

"That was unnecessary to the conduct of business."

"I did it for my own satisfaction."

"You were sent to Lancashire to learn more about the business so that you might serve the company more effectively in the future. You were not sent to ask questions of the miners. If you have any thoughts that run contrary to this sentiment, I suggest that you leave them unsaid."

"I understand, sir. But there is something I wish to say. It is a question, actually."

Murd waited.

"It concerns the conditions that the miners labour under and the wages that they are paid."

"I pay a fair day's wages for a fair day's work. I do not choose the rate. The market does."

"But the rate is low to begin with. And the practice of cutting the workers' pay if they fail to mine a certain amount of coal each week encourages unsafe work habits."

"The miners are not imprisoned. They are free to leave my employ at any time. A cow is worth a certain sum in the market place, and one should not pay more. A miner's labour is worth a certain sum in the marketplace, and he should be paid no more."

Edwin could just as easily have been expressing concern for the well-being of a spider on the wall.

"And consider the times we dig for coal and find none," Murd continued. "The miners are still paid. If we were to increase their pay as you suggest, the cost of coal and everything that it is used for would rise to the sky. Your simplicity is captivating, but I wish it were accompanied by a bit more wisdom."

The latter words were spoken with politeness as cutting as wrath. And their message was clear. The earth had been made for Murd to trade in. Rivers had been formed for the purpose of floating his barges laden with coal. The miners were beasts of burden to be worked so much and paid so little as settled by the laws of supply and demand. Beasts that increased in number by a certain percentage each year. Beasts who were a little pinched when wheat was dear and over-ate when wheat was cheap. Murd thought no more of viewing the miners as individual men and women, each with a separate identity, than of separating the sea into its component drops.

Murd took a small knife with silver trim from his pocket and began paring his nails.

"Let me tell you a story that my father told me when I was a child," he said to Edwin. "Twin sons were born several minutes apart to a king. The older son was destined to rule the kingdom.

The other son was relegated to a life in the shadows. Each of us has a role to play. I am not an alchemist who transforms coal into gold. How do you suppose the coal comes out of the ground? It is enterprises such as mine that cause England to be respected and powerful throughout the civilized world. Can there be harvest without seed? Heat without fire? Can anything be produced from nothing?"

"I understand, sir. But I believe that the conditions the miners labour under are unnecessarily dangerous."

"You are an obstinate young man."

"I prefer to think of myself as principled."

"Are you suggesting that I am not?"

"No, sir."

"Then find other words with which to express yourself."

"Yes, sir."

"The dangers in the mines of which you speak stem from carelessness and drunkenness on the miners' part. In every instance where there has been a fatality in one of my mines, it was determined later by a coroner's inquest that the company followed the law. That is the heart of the matter. We follow the law. A more primitive state of society in which labour asserts itself beyond reason might suit some. But it would not be to my liking, nor would it be in the best interests of England.

"Men of business owe a duty to other men of business to stand together," Murd continued. "Either we control the mob, or the mob will take what we have. There is nothing between fully defending our interests and throwing our fortunes away. You might make a fine politician someday with your lofty parliamentary rhetoric. But that is of no use to me in the conduct of my business."

Murd rose from his desk with his arms folded and looked firmly into Edwin's eyes.

"You are a capable young man with a gift for relating to people. But my patience with you is being tested. There is a disrespectful manner in your words that does not become you and which you must curb. You have done a great deal to raise yourself in life. Do not spoil it. If you are ungrateful for the opportunity that I have given to you, perhaps you would prefer to work in a mine."

Edwin spent much of the next day contemplating his future. As one goes through life, so much is dependent upon external circumstances and the will of others. But there is one aspect of life where a man has complete control, and that is his own morality.

Edwin was unsure how much longer his conscience would allow him to work for Murd. More than ever, he looked forward to seeing Ruby at the learning center on Saturday, spending all of Sunday with her, and conversing together with regard to his dilemma. The wait seemed interminable.

Edwin arrived early at the learning center on Saturday morning and looked round the room. Ruby was not there.

One of the other instructors approached him. A messenger, Edwin was told, had come to the learning center the previous Saturday and given Ruby an envelope. She had opened it and immediately left.

"She has not been here since," the instructor said.

Edwin worried that there was illness. Perhaps Marie had taken sick. He stayed at the learning center for only a brief time, then went to Marie's bakery. I was there when he arrived.

Marie recounted for Edwin what had happened on the previous Saturday.

"Could I have been the cause?" Edwin asked.

"That is not possible," I assured him. "I saw the way that Ruby looked at you when you were together. And she told me of her feelings for you. We thought for the briefest of moments that she might have run off with you. But she was in such torment that we knew it was not so."

"Ruby said that her leave was voluntary," Marie told Edwin. "But she was in such distress that I cannot believe she took this course of her own free will."

"We have talked with the people at the learning center regarding her disappearance," I added. "Octavius Joy has made inquiries on our behalf. All we know is that a man brought a letter to her on the day before Ruby left London. She was in distress when she returned home that afternoon. The following morning, she was picked up by a carriage. We have not seen her since."

Marie wrung her hands. "I am tortured. Why did I not say firmly to her, 'You have no right to these secrets. I demand that you tell me what this is about.'"

A tear, one of many shed since Ruby's departure, crept down Marie's cheek.

"It is not just one loss," Marie said. "It is the loss of the little girl, three years old, entering upon a joyful new life. It is the loss of the child, learning to read, exploring the world that was opening up before her eyes. It is the loss of the loving spirit blossoming into womanhood, excited and in love. And worse, far worse, is not knowing what suffering Ruby is enduring now."

Her eyes took on a haunted look. "I feel very old and alone."

Edwin stayed with us until late that afternoon.

"I strive sometimes to disguise my feelings," he confessed. "But I will tell you plainly that I love Ruby. It will weigh upon me for as long as she is gone that I did not share this feeling with her."

Before leaving, Edwin gave us his address, both at home and at work, so that we could report any news of Ruby to him.

"How soon do you think she will return?" he asked in parting.

"We do not know that she will," I said.

CHAPTER 8

Ruby had never loved London more than when the ties that bound her to it were broken.

A man upon a field of battle might receive a mortal wound and not know how badly he has been hurt. So too, Ruby did not understand at first the full depth of the strike that had been inflicted upon her heart. That knowledge came in a procession of gloom as the shores of England disappeared from sight.

To have committed no wrong and yet to be thrust alone into an alien world, separated from those she loved, when a few days before she had been surrounded by joy, was all but impossible to bear.

She thought of Murd. Did men walking on the street shrink without knowing why when he walked beside them? If he stood above a sleeping child's bed, was the child troubled in its slumber by Murd's dark shadow?

She still did not doubt the tale that Murd and Isabella had told her. She knew now that her love for Edwin was without hope. But still she loved him.

She would have gone to the world's end to be with Edwin. Now, for Edwin's sake, she was going to the end of the world without him.

Ruby was travelling on an oak-hulled paddlewheel vessel with coal-fueled seawater boilers and secondary sail power. The sails hung from iron masts and would help keep the ship on course in rough seas.

It was not a large ship. The vessel had fifty first- and second-class cabins and three hundred passengers crammed into steerage like human freight.

The steerage area was a low dark stifling enclosure filled to overflowing. Bunks were piled one on top of another and lined the sides of the hold. Each bunk was four feet wide, made of rough boards, and the resting place for four people. The roof of the hold was less than seven feet above the floor.

The mother and two children with whom Ruby shared a bunk had lived in Sheffield. Her children were a boy of five and a girl of three.

There were English people, Irish people, Welsh people, Scottish people. All with shabby clothes and boxes containing what was left of their belongings. Men, women, and children swarmed in the dim light.

A baby fed at its mother's breast. In another part of the hold, a slattern girl of twelve seemed as much a grown woman as her own mother. A woman with an infant in her lap mended another child's clothes and quieted one more who was crawling about on the floor. An old grandmother held a sick child, rocking it to sleep in arms as thin as the child's own limbs.

Surrounded by the multitude, Ruby felt very much alone. The other passengers had left England by choice and would arrive in America with optimism and hope. Hers was a different journey.

At the end of the day, preparations for dinner began. The ship provided each passenger with a daily ration of water. Beyond that, they were responsible for their own food.

Ruby hadn't known that.

The passengers had brought bread, cured meat, cheese, and other provisions. Fortunately, the box that Murd's man, Charles, had given to Ruby contained dried food and eating utensils.

Without that, Ruby would have been a beggar.

Then came night. Dark dismal night with no sound but the waves of the sea and, now and then, a crying child lifting up its little head to be kissed by its mother.

Ruby lay on the hard wood bunk, haunted by past hopes and remembrances. She had not known what loneliness was before. She knew it now. It swept through her like a damp winter chill. She was alone in the world with no home and no one to love her. No fairy-tale dwelling surrounded by evil spirits in the heart of a dark forest could have been lonelier than the steerage hold.

The night brought back long-forgotten memories of the hunger and pain that Ruby had endured in the cold damp winters of her early childhood. She imagined herself as she was then, clinging to Christopher's hand. She remembered how she had looked up into his loving face and how his eyes sometimes filled with tears as he gazed upon her.

She had not slept at all on her last night in London. And she had slept little on the journey to Liverpool. She fell asleep now because she was exhausted.

The great voice of the sea rumbled through her sad slumber.

By the second day at sea, Ruby was acquainted with the rules of steerage.

The area around and under each bunk was to be swept by the passengers each morning. The sweepings were then thrown in a large bag and emptied into the ocean.

No smoking of tobacco or any open flame was permitted in the steerage area.

Steerage passengers were required to be in their bunks by ten o'clock each night.

All blankets and other bedding were to be taken on deck and aired twice each week.

No clothes could be washed or hung up to dry in steerage. Every fifth day, washing above deck was permitted.

No cards, dice, or other forms of gambling were allowed.

There were two primitive toilets in the steerage area. Both were always in use with passengers waiting in line.

There was also a cow on board to provide milk for the ship's officers and passengers who were travelling in first class. It occurred to Ruby that the cow was probably receiving better treatment than the passengers in steerage.

When the weather was fair, the steerage passengers went up to the deck, where they were allowed to stand in a certain area and fill their lungs with fresh air. Ruby spent considerable time there and grew friendly with some of the seamen. They were strong men with faces burnt dark by the sun, who had toiled and wandered through all kinds of weather.

Some of the other passengers tried to lift her spirits. One, a stout man from Birmingham, had only one leg, and the popular prejudice runs in favor of two. But he had brought a fiddle with him, and played it tolerably well.

A handsome lad of eighteen had an eye for Ruby. She gave him no encouragement, and he was a gentleman about it.

Not everyone was to be trusted. One of the passengers, it was whispered, was fleeing the law. People kept a close watch on the few valuables they had when he was nearby.

Each day, Ruby saw countless acts of simple kindness. There was more mutual assistance and decency in the unwholesome ark on which she was travelling than might have been found at a gathering of London society.

Faces became familiar. People smiled and talked with her. She helped care for some of the children. They took a liking to her, and she to them. The children gave her hugs and asked that she kiss them. That helped to raise her spirits.

But not enough.

The rising sun heralds a renewal of hope. But for Ruby, the sun each day revealed the vast loneliness of the sea. She would stand against the railing on the deck and gaze at the flat never-ending line of the horizon.

The ocean had looked that way a thousand years before. She thought about the great distance that she was from home, and wondered whether she would ever see London again. All the while, the waves never stopped any more than the earth stops circling round the sun.

Sometimes Ruby took *The Adventures of Oliver Twist* from her belongings, stared at the title page, and read the inscription written for her in Edwin's hand. She read the inscription again and again, feeling sadness and shame for her foolishness in imagining that Edwin might be the handsome young prince who would someday love her.

She treasured the book more dearly than the Bible.

She thought often of her walk with Edwin and the Sunday they had spent together.

There were times when Ruby feared that loneliness would overwhelm her. She dreamed often of home. The walls of the steerage hold would melt away, and things came back as they used to be.

There was a warm fireside and the little supper table. Christopher and Marie were laughing. Then the comfort of the dream would disappear in the cold hard truth of waking.

The ship's captain led a religious service each Sunday. Ruby attended, hoping for solace, but found none.

Twice, in the distance, she saw the sails of ships travelling eastward in the direction of England. Otherwise, her ship was alone on the vast ocean waters.

One of the women in steerage gave birth to a child. She lay down on her back and was attended to by two other women, one of them a midwife by trade and the other a mother with five children of her own.

Two men lifted a blanket to protect the woman's privacy.

There were periodic cries of pain.

"Push . . . Breathe . . . Push . . . Breathe . . ."

Then the cry of an infant.

Towels were doused in boiling water. The woman and her child were washed. The umbilical cord was tied with string and severed with a knife. The blanket that had shielded the woman from view was lowered to reveal an infant wrapped in a towel, lying on its mother's stomach.

"You have a son," the father was told.

By the end of the day, the infant was feeding at his mother's breast. Two days later, the mother was up and about.

There was a death. A old man travelling in steerage with his daughter and her three young children died. One of the seamen built a coffin from crude wood planks. The ship's captain conducted a brief funeral service. Then the coffin was filled with sand. Holes were drilled in its sides, so that it would sink when thrown into the sea.

That night, there was a storm. The evening was tranquil at first, but angry clouds were gathering. The wind picked up.

The steerage passengers were instructed to lie in their bunks and hold tight to ropes tied to the wall. The entrance to the hold and all ventilation openings were closed to prevent flooding. Rain fell heavily soon after. Many of the passengers were made sick by the rolling of the sea. They vomited, and the stench of the unventilated air in the hold grew stronger.

After the storm, more than before, the passengers wished for the journey to end.

"When will we be in America?" Ruby asked one of the seamen.

"Another five days, most likely. We are going along as sensibly as any ship can."

Several days later, a general excitement began to prevail on board. Predictions as to the precise day and even the precise hour at which the ship would reach Boston were freely made. Gamblers among the passengers placed bets on when land would be sighted. There was more crowding on deck and looking out at the horizon than there had been before.

Each morning, there was a packing up of things, which required unpacking each night. Those who had letters of introduction to deliver in America or friends to meet or any settled plans for doing anything discussed their prospects again and again.

Ruby had no idea what she would do when she arrived in Boston. She could have formed an elephant as easily as an intelligent plan for her arrival in America.

Then, on a bright sunny morning, the horizon changed. Land stretched out on either side. One great sensation pervaded the entire ship. The soil of America lay before them.

White wooden houses and wharfs appeared . . . There were noises, shouts . . . Piers crowded with uplifted faces . . . Men and boys running . . . A straining of cables . . . Disembarking . . . On dry land, terra firma.

Ruby Spriggs was in America.

CHAPTER 9

Ruby's ship arrived in Boston in the early afternoon. She disembarked with the other passengers, thankful to be on solid ground. At sea, she had made a compact with herself to not think about what lay ahead until she was in America. Now she was there.

"I must look forward, not to the past," she told herself. She resolved to deal with whatever the future might bring. But she could have fallen from another planet for all she knew of Boston.

The tramp of footsteps and rattle of wheels sounded on the cobblestone streets. Ruby made her way along the crowded wharf with her carry bags in hand. Her clothes, had they been on someone with fewer graces, might have looked a bit shabby.

A boy offered to carry her bags for a small price and take her to an inn where rooms were cheap. They walked a short distance along a street bounded on one side by quays and on the other by a row of storage houses. Before long, they came to an inn with a faded wooden sign beside the door.

A little money will go a long way if sparingly spent. Ruby paid for two nights, hoping that she would find a more permanent residence soon and, more important, a job.

The first order of business in her room was to write a letter to Marie. Pen in hand, she began:

Dearest Marie,

I hope that you will be happy to hear from me. But you will not be half so happy to hear from me as I am to write to you. Your life is as it was before. You miss nothing unless it is me. I miss you very much. Everything in my life is different now.

I have just arrived in America. My health is good despite the rigors of the ocean crossing. I am in Boston, but cannot say with certainty how long I will be here. On the voyage over, many of the passengers spoke of New York. I will write to you again when I am settled.

Please do not think differently of me because of my leaving. It would break my heart should you believe me to be less grateful and loving in any way than I was during all the years that you were so good and kind to me. Remember me as the little girl who you and Antonio protected with so much tenderness and whose cold hands you warmed at your fire.

I think of you both every day with love.

With devotion,
Ruby

The proprietor of the inn told Ruby that mail was shipped from Boston to England pursuant to a contract between the United States government and the Collins Steamship Company. Ruby brought the letter to the steamship office, where it was weighed and stamped "Paid 24 cts." It would be put on a ship to Liverpool before being rerouted by the British postal authorities to London. Delivery would take two to three weeks.

Walking back to the inn, Ruby saw a young man in the distance and thought for a moment that it might be Edwin. She chastised herself that such foolishness must stop.

She passed a market where the food was invitingly arranged, and bought the first fresh fruit and fresh vegetables that she had seen in weeks. In her room, she spread them out on the bed and tried to envision the life that lay before her.

"With one night's unbroken sleep, I will feel better."

A long journey at sea is the best softener of a hard bed. Ruby slept soundly on her first night in Boston. The following morning, she was out and about early. The bright sun made even the dingy old storage houses brighten up a bit. Men took down the shutters on shop windows to reveal the wares inside.

Ruby stopped first at an immigrant hiring office that one of the passengers on the ship had told her about. There were notices on the wall for all kinds of employers wanting all sorts of servants, and all sorts of servants wanting all kinds of employers. A lady of modest means wanted to board and lodge with a quiet cheerful family. And here was a family describing itself in those very words that wanted exactly such a lady to live with them. But when Ruby inquired of the man in charge how meetings might be arranged, she was told that the payment of a dollar was required first. Something in the man's eyes suggested that, were the payment made, it would be an investment without return.

Walking about the city, Ruby saw a sign offering employment in a stable. But she knew more about unicorns than of horses.

She wondered if she might get a job as a teacher.

Then she came to a marketplace with a shoemaker, a tailor, other small merchant shops. And a bakery. She went inside the bakery and told the proprietor that she was from a family of bakers. He had no position to offer. But he liked her manner and knew of another baker who had an opening. By day's end, Ruby had a job.

"But I must have a place that I can call home," she told her new employer.

The baker knew an old man and woman who lived in a small house nearby with a room to let on the top floor.

The old man led Ruby up crooked stairs to a narrow room with a tiny window. The ceiling sloped and, at the foot of the bed, was no more than three feet high. There was a chair with horsehair sticking out of the cushion, a little looking glass nailed to the wall, and a washing table.

They agreed on a price.

When Ruby awoke the following morning, she did not recognize her surroundings.

Ruby liked the customers who came to the bakery, and they liked her. The children who accompanied their parents were particularly disposed to attach themselves to her.

In her free time, she walked about Boston. When the weather was warm, people sat in doorways, strolled in the streets, and enjoyed the serenity of Boston's green places. Ruby asked questions of those she met about America's literature, its system of education, and issues of the day. She was pleased when, on occasion, the conversation turned to Dickens, although that rekindled a longing for home.

At night, Ruby sat sometimes at the open window in her room and stared at the stars. She thought of the loved ones she had left behind in London, and tears came to her eyes. She tried at times to concentrate on the room to take her mind off her loneliness. On the cracks in the ceiling, the flaws in the window glass making ripples and dimples, on the washing table having only three legs. It was to no avail.

She thought often of Edwin. And dreamed of him. It is hard to abandon cherished hopes. When she awoke from her dreams, Edwin was gone. But the sadness she felt upon waking was no worse than her sorrow before sleeping.

"Are dreams and memory not the same?" Ruby asked herself. "Both occurring wholly in the mind."

Edwin, Marie, Octavius Joy, all of us, were far away. There was a wide ocean to be crossed if she was to see us again. Ruby knew that, even if she chose to return to England, it would be a long time before she could accumulate the money necessary for the passage home.

By late June, Ruby had been in America for a month, and the calendar heralded the start of summer. The song of birds filled the air. The public gardens were filled with flowers.

Ruby was walking near the waterfront on one such day, reflecting on her time in Boston. A troupe of acrobats had set up on a pier. There were three pretty women, three handsome men, and six children. One of the men balanced another on the top of a pole. All of the performers danced upon rolling casks, stood upon bottles, and twirled flaming sticks. Every ten minutes, the children were sent into the crowd that had gathered round the performers to ask for money.

A woman, not with the troupe, stood across the street, offering handbills to passers-by. Ruby took one from her:

—TOWN MEETING—
Lucretia Mott
WILL SPEAK TONIGHT AT FANEUIL HALL
"WOMEN MUST BE GIVEN OPPORTUNITIES EQUAL TO
THOSE GIVEN TO MEN."
SEVEN O'CLOCK—ADMISSION IS FREE.

Ruby had become aware during her time in Boston that there was a growing movement within the United States to abolish the enslavement of coloured people in the country's southern and western regions. The handbill spoke of equality of a different kind. She decided to attend.

Faneuil Hall was a large redbrick building near the waterfront. The ground floor served as a market. There was a large assembly room with a balcony on the second floor.

Ruby arrived shortly before seven o'clock. The hall was filled to near capacity with an equal number of men and women. The evening was hot. The windows were open.

At seven o'clock, a woman between fifty and sixty years of age walked onto the stage. Often, women in America were not allowed to speak at public gatherings. The fact that she was speaking at all was noteworthy.

"My name is Lucretia Mott," the woman began. "I was born in Nantucket, not far from here. My husband and I have four daughters and a son and live in Philadelphia. I am speaking tonight to both the women and the men in the audience."

Her voice was firm and carried through the hall.

"It is fitting that we meet in this place. Faneuil Hall has been called 'The Cradle of Liberty.' Samuel Adams spoke here against a tea tax imposed on the colonies by the British and in support of independence from England. Daniel Webster eulogized Thomas Jefferson and John Adams in this hall. I am here to speak with you regarding a similar matter of justice. There is nothing of greater importance to the well-being of this country than the true and proper position of women.

"Women have been denied status equal to men for ages. We are denied the right to vote and cannot hold elected office in any state. We must follow the laws that are made, but we have no say in the making or administration of them. We contribute our share in taxes to support the government, but have no voice in their levying. This is taxation without representation."

"In England also," Ruby thought. "Unless, of course, one is the Queen."

"We are denied a full education," the speaker continued. "The colleges are closed against us. Custom and the law reserve almost all avenues to wealth, including nearly all profitable employment, to men. When women are permitted to work, we receive only scanty remuneration."

The oration continued for almost an hour, delivered with a resolute bearing.

"Too often in marriage, there is an assumed superiority on the part of the husband and an assumed inferiority with a promise of obedience on the part of the wife. This custom, handed down from dark feudal times, is inconsistent with the spirit of enlightenment.

"Once married, a woman is all but dead in the eyes of the law. The law degrades the wife to the level of a slave. In the eyes of the law, marriage makes the husband and wife one person, and that person is the husband. The very being and legal existence of a woman are suspended during marriage and incorporated into that of her husband. There is no foundation in reason for this subjugation. Were women truly the abject things that the law considers us to be, we would not be worthy of the companionship of a man."

There was a murmur of assent from the audience, more from the women than the men.

"We cannot hold property in our own name. A man may file for divorce, but his wife may not. In cases of divorce, guardianship of the children is given to the man without regard to who is the more suitable parent."

A large man stood up in the audience. He was negligently dressed and squarely built. His face was a crooked piece of workmanship that bespoke of obstinacy and dull intelligence. His stomach looked to have been filled many times with ale, including, judging by his carriage, a copious amount of ale that evening.

"Know your place," the man shouted. "If you were less ugly, your husband would not send you out alone into the night like this."

Heads turned.

Lucretia Mott resumed speaking with no loss of composure.

"Sometimes, the effort to discuss the just place of women in society is met with scorn and ridicule. We expect such a response from those who are ignorant. From the intelligent and refined, we expect that gross insults and vulgar epithets shall not be applied. Free discussion of this subject, as with all subjects, should never be feared. Nor will it be, except by those who prefer darkness to light. Only those who know that they are in the wrong fear discussion."

The heckler sat, silent now but unhappy.

"Often, a husband and wife begin life together," Lucretia Mott continued. "By equal industry and united effort, they accumulate modest wealth and a home. If the wife dies, the household remains undisturbed. The husband's shop or farm is not broken up. But if the husband dies, his wife receives only a portion of their joint wealth, and she is dispossessed of that which she earned equally with him. The sons come into possession of the property and speak of having to keep their mother. In reality, it is the mother who is keeping them. Why in the name of a gracious God should such things be?"

At the close of Lucretia Mott's remarks, the meeting was opened up for questions. Most of those who spoke were men.

"You advocate equality for women," a well-dressed man said. "But would not the course that you suggest detract from the respect that men show for the beauty of women and concern for their weaker physical condition?"

"Nature has made us different from men," Lucretia Mott answered. "That is clear in our configuration and our physical strength. We are satisfied with nature. But we deny that the Creator intended the present position of woman to be the limit of our usefulness. Women will not attain the proper place in the Creator's plan until the civil, religious, and social disadvantages that impede our progress are removed."

The questioner pressed his point with emphasis on the homage paid to women.

"That no longer satisfies us," Lucretia Mott responded. "The flattering appeals to feminine delicacy, which too long satisfied us, are giving way to greater recognition of our rights and responsibilities in life. Women should cultivate all of the graces of our sex. But we should not be playthings, content with the demeaning flattery too often addressed to us."

Another questioner rose to his feet.

"It is clear in the Declaration of Independence. All men—not all men and women, men—are created equal."

Lucretia Mott countered.

"The same document eloquently provides that governments derive their just powers from the consent of the governed."

There was another attack, this one more angry.

"You would destroy God's plan. It is in the First Epistle of Paul to Timothy. 'Let the woman learn in silence with all subjection.

Suffer not a woman to teach nor to usurp authority over the man, but to be in silence.'"

"In the beginning," Lucretia Mott answered, "God created men and women, and gave dominion to both over the lower animals but not to one over the other. The laws given to Moses on Mount Sinai for the governance of men and women were equal. Those who read the Scriptures and decide for themselves rather than accept the distorted application of the Bible, given to them by narrow-minded clerics, do not find the distinction that you speak of."

Another man rose to speak. He was uncommonly short, four feet tall at most, with the head of a normal-sized man on a small stubby body and small limbs such that his proportions seemed wrong. His face was covered by a full but well-kept beard. If anything, his head seemed larger than it was, owing to the smallness of his body.

To describe his condition more directly, he was a dwarf.

He looked to be about thirty-five years of age, although Ruby was unsure how men of his condition appeared as they grew older.

"I have a passion for liberty and detest oppression of any kind," the dwarf said.

He had an intelligent face and bright grey eyes. His voice was deep and sounded as though it were coming from one much larger than he was. When he first rose, Ruby had seen him only for his size. Now she noted his dignity of bearing and the eloquence of his words.

"I am unsatisfied," the dwarf continued, "with the division of society into two classes, one of which rules the other by accident of birth. As long as that condition exists, America shall be neither a model of wisdom nor an example to the world."

The drunken heckler rose to his feet again.

"Sit down, Tom Thumb," he bellowed. "Or are you sitting already? I cannot tell."

There was scattered laughter around the hall.

Ruby felt anger welling up within her. Nature had implanted a sense of decency in her breast. She stood and, almost without thought, spoke.

"I dare say, he's more a man than you are."

There was more laughter than before in the hall, this time directed at the heckler.

"And probably twice as smart," a woman shouted.

Sensing that the crowd was with him, the dwarf addressed his detractor.

"Take a word of advice, sir, even if it comes from one who is shorter than you are. Try not to associate a diminutive stature with mental shortcomings. My opinion is worth no more but also no less than that of a full-sized man."

The town meeting ended at nine o'clock. As Ruby left Faneuil Hall and thought back on the evening, she realized that she had forgotten her cares for the first time since leaving England. However briefly, the dull pain of loneliness had been gone.

She was not used to being out this late. There were fewer people on the street than she would have thought. At first, she did not know that she was being followed by a shambling figure. Then she realized that a man was behind her. She quickened her pace. He did the same. When she walked faster, he walked faster. When she lingered, he lingered.

Buildings cast shadows over the road, making the dark night darker.

She was frightened now.

Then the man—and he was a large man—moved to her side and peered into her face with an intrusive leer. His face was rendered more sinister by a tangle of reddish brown hair and thick brows that overshadowed his eyes.

Ruby recognized him as the heckler from the meeting hall. She had not realized before how big he was.

The man eyed her like a wolf. His coarse look frightened her.

"Why do you spend so much effort avoiding me?"

Ruby was unsure whether to go forward or retreat.

"You walk too near. Please, stand back or go on."

"Nay, my pretty one. I will walk with you. Do you think I am drunk?"

"I think that you have been drinking."

He moved in front of Ruby, blocking her way with his legs spread wide apart.

"You might use force," she thought. "But I will resist you with every resource at my command."

He grabbed her arm and held her in his grasp.

"Let go of me," she cried.

"You look pretty in a passion."

"Instantly. This moment."

"Tell me, pretty one. Why are you so proud?"

"Leave me alone."

"You can't hide your beauty from a poor fellow like me. Give me a kiss."

"Let me go."

"A kiss for every cry. Scream if you love me, darling."

Her terror was growing. Then a voice from behind sounded.

"If you value your life, let her go."

The bully turned, still holding Ruby in his grasp.

"This must not go on," the dwarf said.

Aghast by the boldness of the interference, the bully looked at the tiny man with scorn.

"Must not go on?"

"Must not and shall not. Choose your next act carefully. If you choose wrongly, the consequences will fall heavily on your head."

"Be gone, little man."

The dwarf's next words were calmly spoken.

"I'll beat your brains out if you have any, or fracture your skull if you haven't."

The bully let go of Ruby's arm, spat on the ground, and moved menacingly forward.

"You continue at your own peril," the dwarf warned, stepping toward him. "I will not spare you."

Ruby held her breath.

The bully spat on the ground again, then turned and walked away. The dwarf did not move until the aggressor was out of sight. Only then did he speak.

"You were kind to me inside the hall tonight," he said to Ruby. "It was only right that I return the favor. Allow me to walk you home, if I may."

He was more sturdily built than she had realized earlier in the evening. There was a dignity in his face that made it rather pleasant to look upon.

"I would be grateful. Thank you."

She slowed her stride to accommodate his as they walked. They exchanged names: . . . Abraham Hart . . . Ruby Spriggs.

Abraham Hart extended his hand.

"It is a pleasure to meet you, Ruby Spriggs. Although the circumstances of our meeting could have been more pleasant."

"Were you not scared?"

"I was. But so was he. He feared me because I am different. He feared me because he thought there was a reason—a gun, perhaps— that I challenged him in the face of his overwhelming advantage in size. And he feared the humiliation that would follow if a man of my size got the better of him."

At the door to Ruby's home, Abraham Hart reached into his pocket and took out a small card.

"This is the address of my business. I am there six days a week. If I can ever be of service to you, do not hesitate to visit."

After he had gone, Ruby looked at the card:

ABRAHAM HART, PROPRIETOR
BOSTON BOOK EMPORIUM
114 TREMONT STREET

The following morning, Ruby returned to work. The previous night's happenings were very much on her mind. Lucretia Mott had given her much to think about. And she felt indebted to Abraham Hart. It intrigued her that he was the proprietor of a bookshop. And he had saved her from God knows what.

Ruby worked in the bakery five days each week. Sunday and Tuesday were her days off. She had not properly thanked Hart for interceding on her behalf. And he had suggested that she visit him at his shop. On Tuesday, she decided to do so.

Tremont Street was within walking distance of Ruby's lodging. Instead of entering the shop immediately, she stood outside and looked at the window. Dozens of books were invitingly displayed, some turned open to the title page or frontispiece.

She opened the door and went inside. The smell of freshly pressed paper filled the air. Leather too. Rows of books were neatly arranged on shelves.

Abraham Hart was sitting behind a desk. He saw Ruby, rose from his chair, and stretched out his short arms to welcome her.

"I didn't thank you properly for rescuing me," she said.

"If admiring a pretty face were criminal, we should all be in jail," Hart responded. "But people should be treated with respect."

Hart introduced Ruby to a young man named Nicholas, who assisted him in overseeing the shop. Then he showed her his wares.

Uncle Tom's Cabin by Harriet Beecher Stowe was prominently displayed. So were books by Herman Melville, Nathaniel Hawthorne, Edgar Allan Poe, and Washington Irving. There were classics by Homer and Virgil, and works by Cervantes and Dante.

England was well represented. There was Shakespeare, of course. And Dickens. Also Geoffrey Chaucer, Daniel Defoe, John Milton, Jane Austen, Emily Brontë, Robert and Elizabeth Barrett Browning.

And in a corner of the shop, a section for children. Mother Goose, the Brothers Grimm, Hans Christian Andersen. It was good to see these treasures.

Hart had a cordial manner and a kind thoughtful face.

"I am an American," he told Ruby, "so I must ask how you like our country."

She was still getting acclimated to it, she said. But apart from her encounter with the bully—and she had enjoyed the town meeting before the confrontation—everything was well.

They talked about books. Dickens versus "our American writers." Hart told Ruby that he wanted to give her a book. She demurred, but he was insistent.

"Think of it as an investment on my part. If you like it, you will come back and buy more."

Ruby asked which book he suggested, and he gave her a copy of *Uncle Tom's Cabin.*

"It speaks to the issue of slavery. And to the dignity of man."

Ruby thanked him and promised to return.

"And one thing more," Hart told her. "You keep addressing me as 'Mr. Hart.' I would prefer it if you call me Abraham. We are much less formal in the colonies than is the custom in England."

Each Tuesday during the next month, Ruby returned to the bookshop. When the weather was pleasant, she and Abraham took long walks. His legs were a bit crooked and spread apart. But his pace was brisk for a man his size. People gave him friendly greetings as they passed. Children were especially fond of him, perhaps because he gave them little candies that he carried in a pocket.

Their conversations were more about the issues of the day than personal.

"We began our political life in America with two distinct advantages over England," Abraham told her. "First, our history commenced so late in time that we escaped the centuries of bloodshed and cruelty through which you passed. And second, we have a vast territory with not too many people in it yet."

He was curious with regard to the things that Ruby told him about England. He had strong views about religion and a low opinion of most clergy. On one of their walks, he fulminated, "The preachers who strew the greatest amount of brimstone along the Eternal Path are deemed the most righteous. And those who preach the greatest difficulty of getting into Heaven are considered the most likely to get there, although it is hard to say by what reasoning that horrid conclusion is arrived at."

"I believe," Ruby offered, "that if one's religion is in harmony with one's conscience, it should not matter whether those beliefs satisfy anyone else. But I am more ignorant than I might be on matters of religion."

"Your ignorance, as you call it, is wiser than most people's enlightenment."

Ruby felt as though she had a friend.

After several weeks of taking walks together, Abraham invited Ruby to his home for a picnic. He picked her up in a carriage on a Sunday morning, and they rode to the outskirts of Boston. Small cottages dotted the road. Then came larger houses with gardens in front and orchards behind.

Abraham lived in a large old house set amidst oak trees and surrounded by a rough stone wall. Inside, the house was like the home of a normal-sized man, save for the fact that some of the furniture was fit for a child. The mantle above the fireplace seemed to have come from the same oak trees as the ceiling beams and floor. The windows were heavily shaded by branches and admitted a subdued light.

"I love this place dearly," Abraham told her. "I have lived here for my entire life."

The picnic was served in the garden by a housekeeper of normal stature. There was a cold roast fowl, a crusty loaf of bread, sliced cucumber, cheese, and a blueberry tart.

Berries hung from branches like clusters of coral beads.

After lunch, the housekeeper brought a bottle of old sherry and two glasses to the garden. Abraham engaged. Ruby did not.

"We have never spoken of my size," Abraham said.

"Nor of mine," Ruby parried.

He smiled.

"There is a difference. My life has been shaped by my physical stature. In polite terms, I am a curiosity. I have heard far worse. I am educated and, I believe, intelligent. I have feelings, which are frequently abused. I am sometimes ridiculed and scorned."

He seemed to be struggling a bit.

"I am told that I was a serious child. I recall liking to arrange all of my toys in a row."

He paused, as though having difficulty coming to the heart of the matter.

"You may speak freely," Ruby said.

"My parents were of normal size. One can say that it is worse to be the way I am. None would say that it is better. It makes life more difficult. And lonely. These things happen in the world."

The shadow of apple trees splayed across the grass.

"It was in this garden that I experienced the worst moment of my life. One day when I was young, some friends and I were gathered round my mother's knee, looking at a picture of angels that she held in her hand. It was summer. I am certain of that because one of the girls had a rose in her hair. There were many angels in the picture, and I remember the fancy coming upon me to suggest which of the angels represented each child there. Once I had gone through the other children, I wondered aloud which of the angels was most like me. I remember the children looking awkwardly at each other. A sorrow came upon my mother's face, and the truth that I was different from other children broke upon me for the first time. The other children kissed me and told me they loved me just the same. My mother held me in her arms, and I cried. I have long since made my accommodation with the world. But my heart aches for that child. I think often of how he would awake after dreaming that he had grown larger, only to find himself the same and cry himself to sleep again."

Ruby could think of nothing to say.

Abraham looked directly at her.

"Why did you come to America?"

There was a moment of silence.

"Most people come here with the intention of improving their fortune. I do not sense that in you."

"A change in my life was necessary."

"I will not pry, since you seem disinclined to tell me more. But I will always be here to listen. I am older than you are and may, on a few small points, be able to offer guidance should you choose to confide in me. I have told you of my trials. Perhaps, someday, you will tell me of yours."

There was no impertinence in the offer. It was as well intentioned as could be.

"There is wisdom of the head, and there is wisdom of the heart," Abraham told her. "Neither is all-sufficient. You are a wonderful young woman. Know your own worth. You can be nothing better than yourself. That will suffice."

That night in her tiny room, Ruby thought about the day just done. There was a shadow on her heart that told of a sad love story. Sad, but a love story just the same. Something inside of her cried out, "Love him! If he wounds you, love him! If your heart is torn to pieces, love him! Love him! Love him! Love him!"

She took paper and pen in hand and began to write.

My Dearest Marie,

I do not quite know how to tell you what I wish to say. The nights here are very long. I cry sometimes when I am alone. I have been torn from my home and those I love.

The people here are kind. I have a room of my own and a job in a bakery. I would say that I am well, but pieces of my heart are in England.

I dreamed last night of myself as very young girl with patches on the clothes I wore before I knew you. I dreamed also of sitting by the fire with you and Antonio and dear uncle by my side. So you are with me still, though I am far away.

Ruby put the pen down, lifted it up, and put it down again, considering what to write next.

I will tell you the whole truth. Forgive the rambling of my thoughts. They are not easily told.

Ruby then poured out her soul in the relief and pain of disclosure. She recounted being summoned to Murd's home, and meeting with Murd and Isabella. She wrote frankly without concealment of any kind.

I left England because I feared that not doing so would bring misfortune to Edwin. If I did wrong to you and Antonio and others I love, it was in ignorance of the world.

The brightest hopes of my heart were set upon Edwin. I have loved him for every minute of every day since I have known him. I now look upon our time together as a dream—a dream I might marry the man I love—that can never be fulfilled.

I know that I must look for what is right in the world. I cannot let my life grow cold because there came my way a good man who, but for the selfish regret that I cannot call him my own, would, like all other good men, make me happier and better.

If by chance you see Edwin, tell him how much I wish for his happiness, that I will never forget his kind face and gentle manner. Tell him that I am sorry for any trouble that my feelings for him brought upon him.

In all of these foolish thoughts, which I confess to you because I know that you will understand me if anyone can, there is one thought that is never out of my mind. I hope that, sometimes in quiet moments, Edwin thinks fondly of me. I hope he remembers that I exist and, in some way, knows that I love him. If I were to die tomorrow, I would bless him with my last words and pray for his happiness with my last breath.

Your devoted daughter,
Ruby

CHAPTER 10

When Ruby disappeared suddenly from London, it was as though the sun that shone over Edwin had left the sky. He recalled every moment of their time together. Every charm that had enveloped her heightened his despair. He tried at times to smile, but it is difficult to smile with an aching heart.

Every Saturday, Edwin went to the learning center. He felt closer in spirit to Ruby when he was there. On Sundays, he visited Marie and myself, always hoping for news, although I had promised that I would immediately bring to him any word of Ruby's whereabouts. We would sit together in the bakery and talk about all manner of things. A bond developed between us. Marie and I grew increasingly fond of Edwin, and our fondness was returned.

"My heart is given to Ruby," he told us. "Nothing in the world will change that. No one would be more welcome in my life than one who brings me assurance that she is well."

Five weeks after Ruby left home, a letter arrived. We knew now that she was in America. She spoke of being in Boston, but possibly going to New York. She expressed affection and a longing for home, but did not tell us why she had left. There was relief in knowing that no physical harm had come to her. But the ashes of the fire that once warmed Marie's home were grey and cold.

Edwin's distaste for Alexander Murd continued without abatement. Murd radiated civility and charm with men of business who could help him to fresh profits. But he was a different man with others. His voice was harsh as he demanded money that was owed to him or sought to limit what he owed.

Edwin declined an invitation to accompany Isabella to a second opera. That did not keep her from visiting the office and hovering over him on a particularly unpleasant morning.

"How is Miss Spriggs, who I saw you with on the street not long ago?"

"I have not seen her lately," Edwin replied.

"I suppose she has lost interest in you."

"Perhaps."

"Most likely, she has run off with a man more suited to her class."

There was a look of malignant satisfaction in Isabella's eyes.

"In any event, I suppose that Miss Spriggs has made clear her lack of interest in you."

Edwin did not respond.

"I have an intuition in these things," Isabella continued. "I ought to know."

Ought to, Edwin thought to himself. But it is unlikely that you do. There are treasures of the heart that gold cannot purchase. I would not expect you to understand.

Later that day, the office secretary was at his desk, reading letters that he was to open before parceling them into separate piles for distribution. The post had come in heavy that morning, and he had a good deal to do.

A man of middle age entered. He wore a grey outer coat with a narrow collar, black pants, and a waistcoat fashioned from ribbed black silk. His cheekbones were high and prominent, and his cheeks themselves so hollow that he seemed to be sucking them in.

He was in an agitated state.

"My name is Harold Plepman. I wish to see Mr. Murd."

"Do you have an appointment, sir?"

"I am the purchaser of coal for the Hospital for Foundling Children. It is about a matter of payment."

Murd was disinclined to receive the visitor when his secretary announced the arrival.

Harold Plepman sat and waited.

Arthur Abbott, the accountant, went into Murd's office. Several minutes later, he reappeared and approached the uninvited Mr. Plepman.

"You are not to come here. Business of this nature is conducted away from the office."

"I ought to have got more money," Plepman said. He was perspiring in the summer heat.

"You have been well compensated."

"Tell Mr. Murd that I know what constitutes a fair bargain. I wish to make a fair bargain with him."

Abbott went back into Murd's office and closed the door behind him.

Moments later, Murd appeared.

"You will leave now," he told Plepman.

"One hundred pounds is not enough," Plepman said.

"I do not ask. I direct. If you come here again, you will be subjected to criminal prosecution."

A wave of his hand was tantamount to dismissal.

Plepman swallowed hard and left the office.

"It was a misunderstanding with regard to a minor matter," Murd told the employees, all of whom had been watching and none of whom, other than Arthur Abbott, seemed to know what the conversation had been about. "I believe it had to do with a transaction that Edwin handled."

"You are mistaken, sir," Edwin corrected. "I have had no transactions with that gentleman."

Murd frowned and, without more, returned to his private office. Soon after, Arthur Abbott approached Edwin.

"Mr. Murd would like to see you," he said.

Murd was sitting behind his desk when Edwin entered.

"It is not necessary for you to correct me on matters of business."

"I understand, sir. But I have had no dealings with that gentleman, nor do I have any knowledge regarding what his grievance was about."

"It is not necessary that you know. You are not to raise the subject with me or with anyone else again."

"Since you brought my name into the matter, sir, I would like to know what it is about."

"All I desire, Mr. Chatfield, is that it be forgotten. All that you need to do is forget it."

Murd reached for a leather-bound ledger on his desk.

"You talk of books, Mr. Chatfield. This is the most treasured book in my library. It is a delightful book, all true and as real as the gold spoken of in its pages. It is written in my own hand for my own particular reading. None of your storybook writers will ever make a book as good as this."

Murd took a small key from his jacket pocket as Edwin had seen him do before, unlocked the drawer in his desk in which there was another key, and used the second key to open a cabinet. Then he placed the ledger on a shelf beside several similar books, locked the cabinet, and returned to his desk.

"If you had more work to do, perhaps you would ask fewer questions. I would like a memorandum from you by tomorrow morning. You are to summarize what we know at the present time regarding the cost of shipping coal from land that is under consideration for acquisition by the company. I trust that will not be a problem for you."

The timing of the assignment was punitive. Edwin understood that. It meant a long night's work to compile information that Murd, most likely, already had at his disposal. But now was not the proper time for rebellion.

That night, Edwin remained at his desk long after everyone else had left the office. The day's events resounded through his mind.

"I am the purchaser of coal for the Hospital for Foundling Children. It is about a matter of payment. I ought to have got more money."

Harold Plepman was purchasing coal. He should be paying out money, not receiving it.

"Business of this nature is conducted away from the office. If you come here again, you will be subjected to criminal prosecution."

The wheels in Edwin's head were turning. A battle with his conscience followed as he considered the moral ambiguities inherent in what he was about to do.

Perhaps the instant act was wrong, but there were larger ethical issues.

Edwin went into Murd's private office. A silver letter opener in the shape of a sword lay on Murd's desk. Edwin took the letter opener and inserted its point into the crack above the drawer where Murd kept the key to his cabinet.

The lock held firm.

Edwin manipulated the blade again . . . A third time . . .

There was a *click*.

Edwin opened the drawer and, taking care not to disturb its contents, removed the key from its resting place. Then he unlocked the cabinet and took out the ledgers, all the while listening for sounds of danger in the night.

There were four ledgers. He spread them out on Murd's desk and began to read.

Over the next six hours, Edwin explored the mysteries of Alexander Murd's business, dissecting its nerves and fibres. It was all there. A full record of invoices, receipts, percentages on dealings, the distribution of money to third parties. The numbers were plain and clear enough that Edwin, with what he knew of the business, was able to interpret them without difficulty.

The Hospital for Foundling Children was paying far more for coal than similarly situated purchasers, and had been for several years. Within a week of each such purchase, one hundred pounds was transferred to Murd's solicitors to be given to Harold Plepman.

The same lack of uniformity in price, followed by payments to purchasing agents, existed with regard to numerous other buyers of coal.

In other areas of the business—such as amounts paid to transport coal—there were irregularities of a similar nature. Only here, Murd appeared to pay less than the standard amount.

Edwin copied the names and numbers that he thought most important onto paper of his own. Then he placed Murd's ledgers back in the cabinet, locked it, and returned Murd's key to the proper place in the desk. Finally, he closed the desk drawer tight and manipulated the lock shut with the letter opener.

The memorandum that Murd had ordered him to write was hastily written. Edwin would deal with the consequences of its shortcomings in the morning. He extinguished his candle and stole out onto the dark streets of London.

The next day, Edwin arrived at the office at his normal hour. Murd spent most of the morning with the door to his private room closed. Several messengers came and went. With each one, a sense of urgency seemed to grow heavier in the air. Edwin told himself that it was only his imagination.

He had tried his best to restore everything in the desk and cabinet precisely as he had found it. But centimeters matter. The angle of a piece of paper resting on a shelf matters. The fear of discovery grew.

"Mr. Murd would like to see you in his private room," Arthur Abbott told Edwin.

Edwin steeled his emotions for whatever lay ahead.

Murd was sitting behind his desk with a dark look on his face.

"You wished to see me, sir."

"There has been an accident of a serious nature at the Lancashire mine."

A sinking sensation swept through Edwin.

"The extent of damage is unknown at the present time," Murd continued. "Lives have been lost, and the mining of coal has been temporarily suspended. There is a threat of violence and the possibility of action by the miners that might spread to other sites.

"I am sending my solicitor, Albert Diamond, to Lancashire this morning. He will observe and gather evidence for the inquest that is sure to follow. You have a way with people, and you were well received by the miners on your visit to Lancashire. I would like you to accompany Mr. Diamond to Lancashire. You will tell the miners that I have the greatest sympathy for their suffering, but that candor obliges you to affirm that nothing improper preceded the accident. You are of no use to me unless you advance this position. I expect that you will conduct yourself in an appropriate manner. You are to calm the miners, not incite them."

The journey to Lancashire took eight hours.

Edwin had met Albert Diamond briefly on several prior occasions. He was a man of formal bearing with a jutting chin that seemed as though it would facilitate passage through a crowded room.

As the train travelled north, the solicitor explained to Edwin that handling the mine incident would involve a combination of diplomacy and management. At day's end, they came to the mining town. The setting sun glared upon the horizon through a grey haze like a sullen blood-stained eye.

Edwin and Albert Diamond disembarked from the train. There was the same thick air, difficult to breathe, and the same blighted ground. But now, death cast a heavier pall. Grief and urgency were everywhere.

The mine site resembled a deadly battlefield. An explosion had happened. More than one hundred men, women, and children working underground had been swept from the face of the earth, many of them without a moment for penitence or prayer.

Doom hung over the scene, imparting a squalid sickly hue. Men and women exerted themselves with steady courage, hoping to rescue friends trapped underground and to recover the bodies of others. Torches burned all night.

The miners had been working at the end of an upwardly inclined tunnel ninety yards off the main shaft. When a tunnel is on an upward slant, any gas that is present collects in the upper end. The men broke through into the end of another up-hill tunnel. There was a rush of gas. Coal dust flew as luminous sparks. The air became inflammable, scorching all within its reach. There was an explosion. Clothes were burned and hair singed off. Skin and flesh were torn apart.

The whole town had gathered for the rescue effort. Teams of workers had been formed. They dug all through the night and through the next day and through another night, then day again. Digging deeper and deeper into the crust of the earth, carrying timber and rock away, searching for the dead with little hope of survivors.

Bodies were pulled up from the pit. Each time, there was a cry. "Alive or dead?"

Then a hush.

"Some dead. Some alive, but badly hurt."

Night came again. The work of rescue went on. Most of the bodies were scorched, some beyond recognition.

"My dear sweet boy had bright blue eyes and a handsome smile," a grieving mother told the undertaker. "Is he among them?"

"It would be best if she stay away," the boy's father was told. "Let her remember her son as he was before."

The parents of a young man still not accounted for looked at each other with thoughts that they dared not speak.

A father stroked the hand of his dead boy, eleven years old. The suffering mother, her heart breaking, threw herself to her knees and pled with the Almighty to release her from her misery.

Two doctors worked round the clock, amputating crushed limbs of the living and struggling heroically but often in vain to close arteries that their cruel knife had severed.

The local preacher walked among the bodies. It was the business of his life to do so. Sometimes, he was able to go back to a family and say, "I have found him."

Edwin helped in the rescue effort, carrying bodies and stones. Never before had he been present at the precise moment when the breath of life left a living soul. With two others, he carried a man to the hovel that was his home. The room smelled of rot. The walls were dark with soot and grease. A coarse tallow candle cast feeble rays of light.

The man was put on the bed that he and his wife had shared for years. His breathing was thick. He had bitten nearly through his lower lip in the violence of his suffering. The blood that flowed from the wound had trickled down his chin and stained his shirt. It was plain that death was upon him.

His wife sat at his side.

"There is no air here," the man whispered, his voice barely audible. "This place pollutes it. If I could get clear of this dreadful place, even if only to die, I would thank God for His mercy."

"We have breathed together for a long time," his wife told him. She reached out and held his hand in her own.

His eyes were barely open.

"I am worn out. I have been wearing out since the age of ten when I first entered the mines. Thirty years, my love. Thirty years in this hideous grave."

He spoke so faintly that she bent close to hear the sounds his pale lips made.

"It is hard to leave you. But it is God's will, and you must bear it. Promise me that, if you should ever grow rich and leave this dreadful place, you will take me with you to be buried beneath green grass and a blue sky by glistening water. Promise me that you will, so I may rest in peace."

"I promise."

The man relaxed his grasp of his wife's hand. A deep sigh escaped his lips, and a smile played upon his face. Then the smile faded into a rigid ghastly stare.

She spoke his name, but there was no reply. She listened for his breath, but no sound came. She felt for the beating of his heart, but there was none. He was dead, past all help or need of it.

The town reeked with misery and wretchedness. Night after night, death carts filled with rude coffins rumbled by. Children cried, grown men grieved, women shrieked.

The smoke serpents that rose from the chimneys were indifferent to who was saved and who was lost.

Julian White had authorized the payment of five shillings for the bringing up to the surface of each body and transporting it to the undertaker. He and Albert Diamond stayed apart from the suffering as best they could. But they spoke often with the overseer, Jonathan Hunt. And they were plotting.

The first burials were on a Sunday. There had been rain the day before and all through the night. It was hot and muggy. The leaves were soaked and heavy upon the trees.

The bodies of one hundred twenty men, women, and children had been recovered. Nineteen were still unaccounted for. Mothers and fathers, husbands and wives, sons and daughters had all been lost. To supply the heavy demand for coffins, the undertaker had called upon several of the surviving miners who were handy with tools to assist him.

Murd's mining company paid for the coffins, each one having a velvet pall. The church vicar gave the burial ground free.

There was a funeral service in a mouldy old church. Rain fell upon the stained glass windows with a constant weary sound. The preacher spoke of God's love and redemption through Christ.

Edwin was not a believer. He comforted himself now by holding to the faith that nothing innocent or good is forgotten. Those who die continue on in the better thoughts of those who loved them and, through the living, play a part in the redeeming of the world.

His eyes drifted to an elderly woman, who sat with a church Bible open before her.

"She cannot read," Edwin thought. "No one who can read looks at a book like one who cannot."

After the service, the coffins were borne slowly out of the church on men's shoulders. A dead silence pervaded the throng, broken only by lamentations of grief and the shuffling steps of the bearers.

A miner stood in the graveyard, readying the marker for his son's grave. He had just enough learning to be able to spell it out.

A miserably dressed woman sat upon a pile of stones, seeking no shelter from the rain, letting it fall on her as it would. "Lay me by my poor boy now," she wailed.

A weazen little baby with a heavy head that it could not hold up and two weak staring eyes seemed to be wondering why it had been born.

Unidentified bodies were buried in separate coffins, with four coffins in each grave. The undertaker had numbered each body and listed its characteristics in a register. A corresponding number was written on each coffin, and all four numbers were placed on a marker above the grave.

All the while, Albert Diamond and Julian White were gathering evidence for what lay ahead.

Alexander Murd was a man who favored cunning over decency. He practiced trickery within the bounds of the law and more trickery when the law looked the other way. Aided by clever practitioners, he made hard use of his power. Now he was readying for the coroner's inquest.

The duty of the coroner after a mine disaster is to inquire into the causes of the accident and to ascertain whether the pit was worked in a manner that endangered human life.

"We had best get it done quickly," Diamond told Julian White. "Before there is time for misunderstanding to spread."

The inquest began before the last bodies had been raised from the pit. The inquest room was on the ground floor of the courthouse. The furniture was solid with an official look. Several dozen miners were in the spectator pews.

Albert Diamond sat at a table with a bundle of papers consisting of legal documents and notes that he had compiled during the previous week. Julian White and Jonathan Hunt were beside him.

A representative designated by the miners sat at an adjacent table.

Edwin chose to sit in the spectator pews with the miners. "The Queen's gentlemen came here once and said that they would mend things," one of the miners told him. "But they have not. We think that the Queen was not told."

The coroner was a man about forty years of age named Samuel Shaw. He had a fat sallow face and false teeth. Unsightly hair sprouted from his ears. His slovenly attire warranted the inference that personal appearance was low on his list of priorities. Most of us have derived an impression of a man from his manner of doing some little thing. The way he smiles or nods his head or greets another man. Edwin disliked and did not trust Shaw.

The coroner selected twelve jurors for the inquest and stated the case to them.

"Gentlemen; you are impaneled here to inquire into deaths that occurred as a consequence of an event in the Lancashire mine. Evidence will be given to you regarding the circumstances attending that event. After hearing the evidence, you will give a verdict regarding the cause of the event based solely on the evidence heard by you and not according to anything else."

The coroner then read aloud a list of the dead, making a short pause after each name.

The giving of testimony began.

Jonathan Hunt was sworn and examined by the coroner. As the overseer spoke, Edwin put his forefingers together pointing upward and rested his chin on the point.

"Are you the overseer of the mine where the event happened?" Shaw asked.

"Yes, sir."

"Please describe the conditions in the shaft and tunnels."

"We have worked there for about two years, and I always considered it a safe place to work. There was good air. I had no idea of any danger. All ordinary caution was used to prevent any accident."

"So to the best of your knowledge, was the pit clean of inflammable air?"

"Yes, sir. I considered it in perfect safety. The ventilation was good. Fresh air was going round as usual. The misfortune appears to have arisen from the sudden appearance of gas that touched a careless man's open lamp."

"Were the men working with the tops of their lamps on or off?"

"They are ordered to always work with them on. But some men do not listen to what they are told."

The miner's representative rose to cross-examine the witness.

"Is it not true, Mr. Hunt, that, if the colliers do not mine a certain amount of coal each week, they are fined a given amount per basket? And that this penalty, as you are aware, encourages them to work with the tops of their lamps off?"

Albert Diamond rose to his feet.

"I object, Your Honour. The purpose of this coroner's inquest is to determine when and how the deceased met their death, not to instruct an ill-prepared questioner on the workings of the mines."

"The question is foolish," Shaw concurred. "I will not allow it."

The coroner addressed the miner's representative.

"It is not necessary to ascertain how the colliery worked. All that this inquest is charged to determine is how, when, and where the miners died. You are precluded from asking any questions of the witness that do not address these issues. Mr. Hunt has testified that the deaths were ascribable to accident. Pure accident. It is unnecessary for you to imply by your questions that there was some other nefarious cause."

It was clear that the coroner intended to belittle any evidence that did not support a verdict of acquittal. The inquest was a sham, making a pretense of justice as players on a stage might act out, while knowing full well that an unwholesome hand had corrupted the proceedings.

The miners were then allowed to call a witness, a young man named Jermaine Truitt, who had been at work in an adjacent tunnel when the explosion occurred.

"We were at work about two hours," Truitt told the jurors. "Then a rush of wind cut by us and there was a rumbling noise. We put out our lamps and ran toward the shaft. Others came rushing out upon us from the side workings, and all of us ran in the dark in the direction of the shaft. Then we got a sudden giddiness and gasping, and knew we had met the choke-damp. It is a sleepy sickness you feel and sinking at the knees, only it is not the breath of sleep. You are breathing death. I called to those ahead of us to stop. Some of them went on, and down they went. The rest of us hurried back until we came to a place where the air could be breathed. The older ones among us tried to keep order by telling us that our friends on the surface would come soon to help us. But all of us feared another explosion or the advance of the choke-damp that would bring us death. Every minute was torment. After the first hour, I gave up hope and was as bad as the others. I knowed our friends would help us if they could. But could they? I sat there praying and making my last peace with God. And God spared us. Part of the roof of the tunnel we were in fell after the explosion. This shut off the fire and the advance of the choke-damp from us. On the next day, our friends made their way through the ruin and saved us."

"A heartrending story," Shaw declared when Truitt concluded his testimony. "But it is not dispositive in any way with regard to the cause of the incident."

The miner's representative asked to call his next witness.

"How many more do you have?" the coroner demanded.

"Quite a few, Your Honour."

"Mr. Truitt was in the pit. He has spoken for all."

"Your Honour, if you please—"

Shaw cut him off. "I will allow for the testimony of one more miner. That is all."

Ethan Crowl took the witness stand.

"I have sat here and listened to Mr. Hunt tell the jury that the ventilation in the pit was good," Crowl began. "By this, I suppose he means that it was as well ventilated as the rest of Alexander Murd's pits, which is good enough to enable him to get his coal out of the ground but not so well ventilated as to enable us to mine the coal with a tolerable degree of safety."

Albert Diamond objected to the witness's remark. The coroner ordered it stricken from the record.

Crowl went on.

"On the day of the explosion, we were ordered by Mr. Hunt under penalty of losing our employment to work with the tops of our lamps off. We heard a fall of stones in the pit and put the tops back on. Sometimes, we blow out our lamps all together when we hear stones fall. At the very least, when we have concerns, our lamps are locked and made safe. But soon after we heard the fall, we were ordered—"

"Your Honour," Diamond interrupted. "I have endeavored throughout this proceeding to treat the miners with the respect due to them because of their grievous loss. But my patience is being sorely tested by irrational testimony such as this."

"Mr. Crowl," the coroner admonished. "The full, fair, and impartial testimony of Jonathan Hunt has made it clear that . . ."

Ethan Crowl slammed his fist down upon the witness table with full force.

"Keep a watch on your conduct, Mr. Crowl."

"I shall not," Crowl shouted. "I have been dragged over burning coals for twenty years. I was a good enough tempered man once. Some people say they remember me that way. But these bloody mines have forced a change."

"You do not understand me," Shaw warned.

"To the contrary, sir. I understand your kind perfectly well. You hatch nice little plots and hold nice little councils and receive nice little favors from those who represent wealth and power. That is all you do."

"Hold your tongue, sir. There is no fouler imputation against a man than to say that he swore to do justice without fear or favor and then exercised his authority to benefit interests other than the impartial administration of the law. I am of the law. I am styled a gentleman by Act of Parliament and the payment of twelve pounds sterling for a certificate each year. I take pride in the purity of my motives and the correctness of my conduct."

Throughout the inquest, Shaw had been writing his findings on a long sheet of paper. Now he charged the jurors with the instruction that they had heard all of the evidence necessary for them to come to a conclusion.

"Death is as much a part of doing business in the mines as it is in the rest of life," the coroner told them. "Providence has been unwatchful of many individuals who have gained their bread in this perilous employment. This unhappy occurrence might have taken place on any day at any instant of time. For reasons of God's infinite wisdom, inscrutable to the human mind, it was suffered to occur in this place and at this time. No one can suppose that the pit was set fire on purpose. The credible evidence is clear that conditions in the mine were in accord with reasonable standards of safety. I cannot conceive how any person might entertain the slightest doubt upon this case."

He then read to the jurors the findings that he had prepared for them.

"The deceased died tragically in the Lancashire pit. We find the cause of this tragedy to be Accidental Death arising from the explosion of inflammable air, which could not be controlled by human means. It has been made clear by testimony heard to the most ordinary understanding that no human means could have been devised to save the deceased. Clearly, there was no design on the part of anyone to cause the explosion or fire in the pit. We, the jury, express full conviction that there was no want of due care and no bad management on the part of those who oversaw the direction and management of the Lancashire mine."

Shaw directed the twelve jurors to sign the inquest report. Seven members of the jury signed the document with an "X." It is unknown which of the others could do more than sign their name.

"Verdict accordingly," the coroner announced. "Accidental death. Gentlemen of the jury, you are discharged. Thank you for your service."

In the aftermath of the inquest, miners milled about angrily in front of the courthouse.

"The coroner himself chose the jurors," Crowl fumed. "No other verdict could have been expected."

"I would have him branded on the face, dressed in rags, and cast out on the streets to starve," another miner declaimed.

"I would shoot him through the heart if he had one," a third miner offered. "Death has no right to leave him standing while it takes our people down."

"The problem is not Shaw," Crowl told the others. "He is only a tool for those in power. If he died today, he would be replaced tomorrow by another just as bad as he is."

Edwin left Lancashire by train the following morning. Crowl was at the train stop to bid him farewell.

"If we lay dead at the bottom of the deepest hole in the earth, rotting in a giant coffin, we would not be less heeded than we are here," he told Edwin. "And there is no way out. If one of our men has an angry word with those who oppress us, to jail with him. If a boy comes of age and tries to live elsewhere, he is a vagabond. To jail with him. If we refuse to work, crowds of young boys and girls growing up in this town would come forward, anxious to take our place and toil in the mines at Murd's pleasure. He need not be afraid of losing his fortune."

Albert Diamond had chosen to remain in Lancashire for another day to finalize some dealings with Julian White. Edwin was alone with his thoughts on the train ride home.

When men commit an injustice, it is not uncommon for them to express pity for the object of their misdeed and to feel virtuous and morally superior to those who express no pity at all. To give Alexander Murd and his conniving instruments their due, they eschewed that sort of dissimulation.

It was easy for Albert Diamond and Julian White to excuse their conduct. "We are men of business. We have a fiduciary obligation to Alexander Murd and a business obligation to fulfill." Jonathan Hunt and Samuel Shaw had their own self-justifying rationale.

As for Murd, his hopes, joys, and affections all melted down to gold. Wealth, and only wealth, was the source of his happiness. Wealth was to be acquired by any and all means. He had no pity for others and no passion but love of coin.

Crafty avarice grows rich. Honest labour remains poor.

"I am uncomfortable when people have power over me," Edwin thought to himself. "I can only begin to imagine what the miners feel."

He knew now what he had to do.

❦

On his first day back in London, Edwin readied his courage to confront Alexander Murd. He would not raise the issue of what he had learned by surreptitiously studying Murd's ledgers. That was for another time. For now, conditions in Lancashire were enough.

In mid-morning, Edwin knocked on the door to Murd's private room.

Murd looked up from his desk when Edwin entered.

"I must speak with you, sir."

"I am busy now. We will talk later in the day."

There was boldness in Edwin's manner.

"Later will not do. I must trouble you to speak with me now."

A look of aggravation crossed Murd's face.

"You are to do as I say, not the other way round. That is my right as your employer and a reasonable return for the advancement that I have given to you."

Edwin did not shrink from Murd's glare. He stood with the strength of a man who had sufficient reply in reserve and was about to deliver it. Then he spoke, looking Murd straight in the eye.

"The plainness of my purpose empowers me to speak. I would like to begin with conditions in Lancashire."

Edwin then spoke from the heart about the mine disaster. A responsible member of human society would likely have listened with horror. At the very least, there would have been an expression of sympathy for the sufferers.

Murd's face showed only indifference and the absence of guilt, as if there were no more spots upon his soul than on his pure white linen shirt.

"Do not talk of disaster in that way. We have nothing to do with disasters in this office."

"A tragedy, perhaps?"

"There are hazards in all occupations. Ships sink to the bottom of the sea, and scores of men are lost."

"In Lancashire, women and children are among the dead."

"What of it?"

"That is illegal, sir."

"The coroner's inquest found no impropriety in the operation of the mine."

"Women and children, sir."

A look of contempt flared in Murd's eyes.

"Is the death of a mother any worse than the death of a father? Is the death of a child half so bad as the death of the grown man who provides for all of the children?"

"It is not just that they die, sir. It is the way they live. There are thousands of miners breathing heavily now, who live in the most degrading poverty and have no chance at a better life. They live lives of unremitting toil—"

"What else are they made for?" Murd interrupted. "Without their toil, their lives are of little worth."

"Not to you, perhaps. But they are precious to those who live them."

Murd looked at Edwin with a cold careless smile.

"You assume a tone of high-mindedness that is most unbecoming."

"I take my position on principle."

"As do I. The people you speak of so lovingly are little better than savages."

"I do not understand your meaning, sir."

"That surprises me because you are usually quick of mind. But I will be plainer. The miners and their families live like beasts.

They are crude. They wallow in filth. They procreate without thought."

"The conditions in which they live are not of their choosing. Perhaps those you disparage would be more to your liking if they were allowed an education and taught to read and write."

Murd's face darkened.

"If the miners learn to read and write," he said in a cold hard voice, "it would be easier for troublesome ideas to spread. And if the miners become educated as you suggest, who would bring the coal out of the ground?"

Murd's visage tightened. Every line in his face was cruelly compressed.

"The rule of my life is to not allow myself to be thwarted by anybody. Anybody. Everyone profits from the neediness of others. Men of business build our fortunes on the weakness of mankind. I am reviled and threatened every day by one man or another, and things roll on just the same. I do not grow poorer either."

"You are immoral, sir."

"Your opinion is of no interest to me."

"Perhaps not. But I do not regret having voiced it."

"You talk like a child."

"My comfort is that I am speaking the truth. Truth that should have been spoken long ago."

"You are an impudent young man."

Edwin weighed his next words.

"Have you ever been in a mine?"

"I decline to answer that question."

"You decline?"

"Your impertinence will not be tolerated."

"Where, sir, are the graces of your soul?"

Throughout the conversation, Murd had conducted himself in an imperious manner. Now his features grew even more forbidding, and he spoke as coldly as if he were made of snow.

"I have been much too lenient with you. You are dismissed from your employment immediately."

"That fits well with my intentions."

"You will be sorry for this."

"I will never regret the preservation of my self-respect, nor will I sacrifice it at your bidding. I am young and the difficulties of my situation have kept me in check for far too long. But I have been roused now beyond all endurance. I would be sorry forever and would despise myself for every hour of my life if I remained in your employ after what has occurred."

"You will leave instantly."

"I will, sir. With the greatest of pleasure. You have not the man to deal with that you think you have."

⁜

And so it was done. Edwin was now a young man with much to offer in the way of ability and personal appeal but without an employer.

There was his future to think of. And redress for the miners. Ruby also weighed heavily on his mind.

His boldness in confronting Murd had obscured the absence of a longer-range plan. Now, Edwin realized, he needed the advice of one wiser and more worldly than he was. He had met Octavius Joy only once, but had been impressed by the older man's acuity and generosity of spirit. Ruby had spoken fondly of him.

The sun was setting when Edwin appeared at Octavius Joy's door. He stated his purpose to the housekeeper and was brought in to see Mr. Joy.

Octavius Joy was at his desk, wearing a comfortable old coat. He rose and greeted Edwin warmly.

"Could I have a moment of your time, sir?"

"As many moments as you wish. Have you any word of Ruby?"

They discussed what they knew. That Ruby was in America and, for a while at least, had been in Boston.

"But that is not why I have come," Edwin said. "I am fighting my way against difficulties and would be grateful for any guidance that you can give me."

Edwin then recounted for Mr. Joy the history of his employment with Alexander Murd, and told him in detail of the disaster in Lancashire and the inquest that followed.

"Upon my most moderate calculation, more than two hundred people have died in Murd's mines within the past ten years. That is a blood sacrifice and an unacceptable price for the miners to pay for their employment."

He told Octavius Joy about general conditions in the mines and the fact that Murd still directed women and children to work underground as labourers.

"And there is one more matter, sir. I am a bit shamed by the source of my knowledge, but I know with certainty the truth of which I speak."

Edwin then told Mr. Joy about his study of Alexander Murd's ledgers and the payments that should not have been made.

"Last night, after returning from Lancashire, I took time to review my notes. There was reference to two earlier payments made to Samuel Shaw in the amount of three hundred pounds each. I would expect that, before long, there will be another disbursement to Mr. Shaw."

"From what you have told me," Octavius Joy said, "I would be surprised if there were not."

Mr. Joy adjusted his spectacles and, after a moment's pause, spoke.

"It is as difficult to stay a moral infection as a physical one. Greed spreads with the rapidity of the plague. Too often in the world of business, there are unlawful partnerships of convenience and mutual interest. All good ends can be worked out by good means. Any goal that cannot be so achieved should be left alone.

"I am familiar with Murd," Mr. Joy continued. "I knew him casually when we shared membership in a club that I belonged to long ago. He is of a class of men that I do not admire. We have different visions of how the world should be. I believe in better things."

Octavius Joy rose from his desk and paced back and forth in thought.

"I like to think of myself as a benevolent man," he said at last. "But I am also stubborn. And I am greatly disturbed by what you tell me. Will you testify to these things in court if need be?"

"I will."

"Give me time to think about these matters. Come back in two days. We will have breakfast together, and I will have a satisfactory answer for you. Almost always, greed overreaches itself."

That night, Edwin was unable to sleep. He closed his eyes as if to coax himself to slumber, and tossed first on one side and then the other. After several hours of tumbling about, he concluded that it was of no use, rose from his bed, and walked about his quarters.

The quiet interval between night and morning arrived. Darkness grew pale and faded away, giving birth to another day. A streak of light widened and spread over the horizon, turning the sky from grey to more vibrant colours.

Edwin walked about London alone with his thoughts for much of the day that followed. He was preparing dinner in his quarters that evening when I knocked on his door.

"We have received another letter from Ruby," I told him. "It explains everything."

CHAPTER 11

When the Inland Office in Liverpool receives correspondence from a foreign country that is addressed to a recipient in London, it forwards the correspondence to the London Office.

London, in 1853, was divided into seventeen postal sections, then into subdivisions, and finally into districts. Once a letter arrived in a district, it was handed over to one of many carriers, who arranged it with other letters as he saw fit and delivered it on a walk.

I will always remember the emotions caused by the arrival of Ruby's first letter from America. But those feelings were trivial when compared to the emotions roused by the arrival of her second letter. Marie and I agreed that I should bring it immediately to Edwin.

Edwin took the letter from my hand and, with his own hands trembling, began to read. He had not gone far when his colour changed. To describe the look that passed over his face would require a new language. He read slowly, hearing Ruby's voice in every word.

The cause of Ruby's flight was now fully understood. Edwin's anger over Murd's grotesque conduct toward her was no small matter. But it was miniscule when set against his sadness for Ruby's hardship. He saw now the sacrifice that she had made and the suffering that she had endured in what she believed was the service of his happiness.

He read the letter through several times.

"That I should love her is no wonder. But that she should love me . . ."

He put the letter to his lips and kissed it, then turned to me and asked, "May I keep this?"

"Certainly."

Edwin folded the letter carefully and put it in his pocket.

"I am appointed to see Octavius Joy tomorrow," he told me. "It is about another matter, but this will take precedence. Ruby's address is on the envelope. We know now where she is. Rest assured, I will spare no effort to ensure that she is brought home safely."

The following morning, as planned, Edwin met with Mr. Joy. As the first order of business, he gave him Ruby's letter.

It would require a painter—and no common painter at that—to depict Octavius Joy's face as he read what had transpired. It is a wonder that the indignant flames flashing from his eyes did not melt his spectacles.

"It sets my whole blood on fire," he said when the reading was done. "Murd has tampered cruelly with an innocent young woman, and he shall be called to account for it. We will deal with Ruby's well-being later today. But there is another matter that we must tend to first.

"I have set up a meeting with Murd," Mr. Joy continued. "By letter that a messenger delivered yesterday, I requested to speak with him. He responded that I should visit him at his home at noon today. I doubt that his choice of venue is an expression of hospitality. Rather, he knows my views on matters of ethics and would prefer to keep me away from his business office. He is unaware of our relationship, but I would like you to come with me."

Octavius Joy folded his spectacles into their case and put them in his pocket.

"Let us go see Mr. Murd. Once we are there, allow me to dictate the order of the conversation."

A servant brought Edwin and Octavius Joy to Murd's study when they arrived at his home. Murd was seated at his desk, encased in the cold hard armour of his arrogance. He did not rise to shake hands, offering instead a nod of his head that rustled his stiff cravat.

He could not have been pleased to see Edwin with Mr. Joy.

"It has been many years since we were in each other's company," Murd said to Octavius Joy, beginning the conversation. "I hope that you are well."

"I am," Mr. Joy answered.

Murd ignored Edwin and gestured for Octavius Joy to sit. Mr. Joy took a chair opposite the desk. Edwin sat beside him. He wondered if this was the chair in which Ruby had sat when Murd and Isabella crushed her heart.

"You asked for a meeting," Murd began. "And I have obliged you."

"I appreciate your finding time in your busy schedule to accommodate me. I believe that you know Mr. Chatfield."

"I do. He was dismissed from my employ several days ago. I assume that this is not a social call, so let us dispense with pleasantries. What business brings you here?"

"I will be brief."

"I am delighted to hear it. It will save us both the wear and tear of a long explanation."

There was no anger in Octavius Joy's face. But his look was one of determination, and he spoke with an air of authority.

"I am concerned first with the operation of your mines."

A modicum of concern flickered across Murd's face. His command of expression could not suppress it. He looked steadily at Mr. Joy, but did so as one is wont to do when he has doubts that what he is about to say will be fully accepted as truth.

"Your statement implies dishonour, and I reject it."

But he seemed to shrink a bit from Octavius Joy's cold, hard eye.

"There are women and children working underground in your mines, some of them for as much as twelve hours a day. That clearly violates the law. Indeed, all of your miners labour under conditions that are unlawful."

"Do not tell me how to run my business. It is mine, not yours."

"The common welfare is my business."

"Exquisitely noble," Murd mocked. "My dear Mr. Joy. You are a wealthy man and deservedly held in high esteem by some of the less fortunate men and women of London. But I am the best judge of my own affairs. Do not be so audacious as to trifle with me."

"I do not trifle. You know me better than that. I am also aware of a pattern of bribery that you have engaged in."

Murd rose from his desk and crossed to the door to make certain that it was shut, then returned to his chair.

"I am not sure that I understand what you are saying."

"I will put the case in a perfectly plain way," Octavius Joy responded. "Illegal payments have been made to agents who contract on behalf of various entities such as hospitals and schools for the purchase of your coal. Illegal payments have also been made to agents who represent the sellers of services that you buy and to certain judicial authorities. I will be more specific with regard to names, dates, and the amounts of payment at an appropriate time."

For the first time since the meeting began, Murd looked at Edwin. Then he returned his attention to Octavius Joy.

"There are times, sir, when honest indignation will not be controlled. I do not know what child's tale Mr. Chatfield has told you. But if this is his plot to ruin me, I shall not sit idly by. I will tell you frankly that the reason for Mr. Chatfield's dismissal was the discovery of financial improprieties on his part."

"I doubt that very much," Mr. Joy replied. "I am sure that Mr. Chatfield brought credit to your company and, I dare say, improved your reputation."

Murd cast as evil a glance at Edwin as could come from his dark eyes.

"And he made inappropriate advances toward my daughter, Isabella, in the hope of working his way up the ranks of society."

Octavius Joy reached out and put a steadying hand on Edwin's shoulder.

"Later," he told Edwin. Then he turned back to face Murd. "Let us proceed with the business at hand. I have stated my concerns. What is your response?"

"We are both men of business," Murd said, seeking a common ground. "We need not publish our disagreements."

"You and I are not alike."

"All men are fortune hunters to one degree or another. The law, the church, the stock exchange, the royal drawing room, Parliament. They are all crowded with fortune hunters, jostling each other in the pursuit of gold. I have my opinion of you, and you have your opinion of me. It is not necessary that our opinions collide at the present time."

"I am giving you the opportunity to explain your conduct in a way that satisfies me that you had no intention of wrongdoing and have conducted yourself within the boundary of the law. If you are unable to do so, I will bring these matters to the attention of the authorities at the highest level."

Murd put his hand to his throat and moved his neck from side to side as though his cravat were troubling him.

"This is a foolish game. Where is the good in it? Come, let us arrive at a settlement. Perhaps a generous contribution to your learning center."

"I have no inclination to bargain with you. And since I advocate the interests of others, I do not have the right."

"Come, we must make a treaty of this. The payments of which you speak were, at worst, lapses in arithmetic."

"Lapses in judgment are more likely. I have seen much business done on sharp practices in my day. But this is a particularly unflattering and unlawful portrait."

There was perspiration now on Murd's brow and an anxious look in his eyes. He turned and spoke directly to Edwin.

"There is no case without you. What sum of money will you set against your silence?"

"No amount is large enough," Edwin answered. "You may read the Lord's Prayer backward if you wish. It will not change what you have done."

Octavius Joy smiled. "You are accustomed to dealing with men who are for sale. This young man cannot be bought."

"A word of reason, sir. This young man, as you call him, tried to extort money from me."

Octavius Joy put his hand again on Edwin's shoulder.

"Perhaps you would like to respond to that allegation and speak to other matters."

Edwin looked directly at Murd and chose his words carefully.

"I would not mind your hypocrisy half so much if you had done wrong only to me. I might even believe that you found justification in your mind for your exploitation of the miners on the thought that you are as immoral as you think you need be in matters of business. But there is more. We know now what you did to Miss Spriggs. The whole sordid scheme has been revealed."

Murd sat silent.

"I wish to know, sir, whether you destroyed letters that were entrusted to you by Miss Spriggs and myself for delivery between us."

Murd looked down with his eyes fixed on his desk.

"You have heard my question, sir. What answer do you make?"

There was more silence.

"Which chair did Miss Spriggs sit in when you tore her heart apart? Your cruelty is enough to embitter Heaven itself. I know your true character now, and I despise it."

Now Murd heard Octavius Joy speaking.

"I have known Miss Spriggs since she was three years old, and I am exceedingly fond of her. No punishment that our laws provide is worthy of being set against the outrage that you perpetrated against her. I doubt you thought for even a moment what that innocent young woman's suffering would be.

"I have tried to separate in my mind your business dealing from your conduct toward Miss Spriggs," Mr. Joy continued. "I have thought of what I would do if you took this course with regard to our discussion of the mines. What remains now is for me to do it. I am not easily diverted from a task. When I say I will do a thing, I do it. There is truth and justice to be found in this matter. I will urge the authorities to find it."

A touch of arrogance returned to Murd's face.

"My legal advisors, as they have done in the past, will prepare my defense against any charges that you make. I will fight you with every resource at my command. I am not a man to be taken lightly."

"Nor am I, sir. Nor am I. You will find that my resolution is as hard as marble."

Octavius Joy rose from his chair. Edwin followed his lead. There would be no handshake in parting. But one more matter remained to be addressed.

Edwin looked scornfully at Murd.

"I would be remiss, sir, if I did not say one thing more. There is a matter you alluded to earlier that I wish to discuss. I believe you suggested that I made inappropriate advances toward your daughter with an eye toward elevating myself through marriage."

"That is correct."

"It is not correct. It is false. Your daughter is an ungainly, stupid, unattractive beast. I view her with loathing and disgust, and have since I first set eyes upon her and heard her whining, unpleasant voice."

"That is quite enough."

"I will finish the thought. You and your daughter are the falsest, meanest, cruelest, most sordid, shameless creatures that crawl upon the face of the earth. You are supernaturally disagreeable and the most grotesque pairing of father and daughter that I can imagine."

Murd ground his teeth together.

"The fertility of your mind in finding ways to insult me is astonishing."

"I am not finished. There is more. The most abject poverty and most wretched condition of human life would be happiness compared to what I would endure were I to marry your daughter and have you—I gag at the thought—have you as my father-in-law."

"The less we say, the better, I think."

"No! The more we say, the better, I think. Of all the women on the face of the earth, your daughter is the last that I would choose to be with. I have not one wish or hope connected with her other than to never lay eyes on her again. Miss Spriggs may not be your daughter's equal in birth according to the customs of society. But she is worth a million of you and your odious, vile daughter and would remain so if she swept the streets for her daily bread while you and your daughter splashed mud upon her from the wheels of a chariot made of pure gold."

As Octavius Joy and Edwin left Murd's home, Mr. Joy's face relaxed and became so pleasant again that Edwin was emboldened to give him a hug.

"The absence of a soul in a living man is far more terrible than in a dead one," Mr. Joy said, reflecting on the hour just passed. "The best I could wish for Murd is that he come someday to be ashamed of what he has done. But that is unlikely. He has no more humanity in him than a stone."

"I feel the fool for having trusted him," Edwin uttered.

"We must always be trusting. Trust and love walk hand in hand, but we must learn whom to trust." Octavius Joy put an arm around

Edwin's shoulders in an enveloping embrace. "Let us go back to my home. Then we will speak about what to do next."

Mr. Joy's housekeeper had prepared a light lunch, which the two men ate in the study.

"The dexterity of lawyers allows these things to happen," Octavius Joy told Edwin. "And in this instance, the dexterity of lawyers shall end them. I will speak with my solicitors tomorrow with an eye toward putting Murd's actions in context and bringing them to the attention of the authorities at the highest level. I am not without influence."

"I would be grateful."

"It is my obligation," Mr. Joy responded. "There is a responsibility upon members of a civilized society to curb the excesses of those who drive the bargain of gold against human life. If the laws of England are honestly administered, Murd will be in prison when this is done. I will do everything in my power to accomplish that end. Murd has sown this. Now he shall reap what he has sown."

The housekeeper cleared away the dishes from their lunch and brought in a pot of freshly brewed tea.

"A man's breath is often shorter but never longer as he ages," Octavius Joy said to Edwin with a smile. "It is a consolation of sorts that I find myself growing wiser as I grow older. Beyond that, at my age, I strive simply to be cheerful and self-reliant."

Mr. Joy poured two cups of tea.

"There is another matter that I wish to discuss," he said.

Edwin waited.

"When I was a young man about your age, the whole of my life was devoted to business and the pursuit of wealth. I was fortunate in worldly matters. Many men worked harder than I did and did not succeed half as well. Then I had an awakening.

I came to understand that we are all responsible for the well-being of our fellow man. And the greater a man's wealth, the greater his responsibility. From that time on, the happiness of others and the advancement of the downtrodden has been the foremost pleasure of my life. I shall never regret devoting my fortune and my years to this cause. I have done some good and, I trust, little harm.

"A long day's work remains to be done in the way of education," Mr. Joy continued. "There is shameful neglect of the children of the poor in England. If the government fulfilled its duty at the beginning by taking these children off of the streets while they are young and teaching them to read and write, these children would become a part of England's glory rather than the shame of our nation.

"I am growing older. We all are, to be sure. But I am much closer to the end of my days than to the beginning. It is time that I planned for someone to assist me in whatever time I have left on this earth and to carry on my work after I am gone. If I searched through all of England, I could not find one more suited to this task than you are. I see great qualities in you. You are meant to do great things. I would like to employ you."

"I am honoured," Edwin answered. "It is something that I would like very much to do, but I cannot do it now. I must go to America for Ruby."

Octavius Joy put on his spectacles, took his checkbook from a desk drawer, and began to write.

"I am employing you now," he said, handing the check to Edwin.

"I cannot accept this, sir."

"But you must. It is a condition of your employment. The amount is sufficient to cover your passage to America, a month there, and return passage for two. As your first assignment, I charge you with the responsibility of bringing Ruby safely home to England."

There was something so optimistic in Octavius Joy's manner that Edwin's spirits soared under its influence.

"Thank you, sir."

"I have great fondness for the two of you and a desire that you be happy together. In time, all will be well."

"How can you know?"

"It is natural and right that you be together. There is a destiny in these things. It will happen as it is meant to be."

CHAPTER 12

Ruby mailed the letter in which she poured out her heart to Marie the day after she wrote it. She knew that roughly three weeks would pass before it arrived in London. And three weeks more before she might receive a reply.

If the letter arrived in London.

It was a leap of faith to believe that a chain of unknown people would take a small piece of paper written in her hand and deliver it to a small bakery in a distant part of the world.

If the letter arrived, Marie would show it to Antonio. Would they bring it to Edwin?

Ruby hoped that they would. Love can thrive in memory on slight and sparing food. It was impossible for her to think of Edwin without loving him. Often at night, she awoke from her sleep and thought of him with a hopeful spirit as if he had been whispering to her in her dreams.

One night, Ruby dreamed that Christopher was sitting at her bedside. Seeing that she had opened her eyes, he bent down and kissed her. "I have come to tell you how happy I am that you are home again," he told her. "Marie, Antonio, Edwin, and I have been wearying so for your return." Then Ruby awoke to reality and the drops of summer rain on the window of her tiny room.

Throughout the summer, Ruby went about her life in Boston. Once each week, she visited with Abraham Hart. She looked forward to those occasions. He took her for lunch. They shared long walks. Each time that Ruby finished reading a book that Abraham had given to her, he gave her a new one.

"I would like to take you to a special place," Abraham told her when they met one sunny morning.

A carriage brought them to the edge of a wood fragrant with wild flowers. Stately oaks rose toward the sky from ground that had never been ploughed.

Abraham led Ruby through a thick green wood. Majestic trees, some with gnarled trunks and twisted boughs, stood in beautiful confusion. Other trees, which had been subdued months before by blasts of winter wind, had not tumbled fully down and lay bare in the leafy arms of survivors, as though unwilling to disturb the general repose by the crash of their fall.

Ruby and Abraham walked side by side. There were times when his short legs put him at a disadvantage in climbing over a fallen tree or jumping from rock to rock across a stream. But he had trod this path many times and was very much at ease.

His mood was cheerful.

"There is an old story," he told Ruby. "It is about a man who, when asked if he could play the fiddle, answered that he was sure he could but did not know with absolute certainty because he had never tried."

Ruby laughed, and they continued on.

At last, they came to a waterfall. Foaming water danced from crag to crag and from stone to stone, sparkling in the sun. Ivy and moss crept in clusters around the surrounding trees.

"I have a liking for this spot," Abraham told her. "I visit it often when the weather is fair."

Ruby's eyes grew moist. The trees were whispering to her that Edwin was not with her, and this was a moment that should be shared with him. She turned her face so that it was hidden from view. But Abraham could see that she was weeping.

He reached up and put his hand on Ruby's shoulder, not as one who would be her lover but with love.

"We have been friends from the start, have we not?" he said.

"We have."

"And we shall be friends in the future. So neither of us should mind the other speaking freely. I asked you once why you came to America. And you gave me no answer."

"I have longed for home till I am weary in my tears."

"Then why did you leave?"

"And if I should tell you everything?"

"I would listen as your friend. We need never be ashamed of our tears."

So Ruby poured out her heart, and recounted all that had happened. She told of her life from the beginning and how, as much as life itself, she loved Edwin.

"To the last hour of my life, he will be part of me. I love him so dearly that I am willing to suffer for him, even though he does not know of my pain. There is a vision of Edwin in my mind. It is always with me. A vision of what I might have been to him and he to me, if only he had loved me. I would not have the memory of Edwin taken away for anything that life can give me. But I love the memory of him too deeply to be happy. What is left of my heart is in England."

The rays of the sun fell upon the water. Ruby and Abraham sat on a large rock just beyond reach of the spray. A lonely princess and a good elf in a fairy tale might have sat and talked as they talked that day and looked very much like them.

"Let me ask you a question," Abraham said. "You have told me what you feel for Edwin. What did Edwin feel for you?"

"It was foolish of me. But I thought perhaps he might love me or that such love might grow someday."

"I do not want to hear 'perhaps' or 'might.' Did you feel in your heart that Edwin loved you?"

"I did."

"Tell me of Edwin's character."

"He is kind and good and caring."

"You know the purity of your own heart. Would you give it to one whose heart was less pure than your own?"

"No."

"Did you confront Edwin and give him an opportunity to speak to the horrible things that were told to you by Murd and his daughter?"

"No."

"And it was arranged by those two so you could not. Instead, you were exiled to America, willed away like a horse or dog."

"I felt perhaps that it was God's will."

The sun had moved behind Abraham, casting an image of him the size of a giant upon the ground.

"You fall into the common mistake of attributing to God matters for which He is in no way responsible. A God who sought to tear you away from Edwin would be an idiot."

Ruby looked upward toward the sky.

"Perhaps it would be better if you did not call God an idiot."

"I did not call God an idiot. I said that, if God did a particular thing—and I do not believe that He did—then His wisdom would be called into question. Love is the most beautiful of the Almighty's works. But like many of His works, it relies upon the assistance of mortals for implementation."

Abraham rose from the rock and stood above Ruby so that she was in his shadow.

"When I was a boy, I liked to pretend that I saw images in the flames from the logs burning in the fireplace. My imagination entertained my parents and myself. Shall I tell you what I see in the fire of your heart? I see a heart well worth winning and well won. A heart that is strong and true. It makes far more sense for you to pursue the happiness you dream about than to shut out the possibility of your dream coming true."

"And what if my thoughts of a life with Edwin are all a foolish dream?"

"You talk of love. I will tell you what love is. It is trust and belief in the person you love against the whole wide world. If you love Edwin, you will believe in him."

A gentle breeze filtered through the leaves, whispering its assent.

"Go back to London. Follow your heart. It is in England with those you love."

Abraham's words were spoken with such conviction and so mirrored Ruby's hopes that she could not doubt them. But even as her spirits rose, reality brought them down.

"I have no money to return to London."

"Money is not a problem."

"It is, since I have none."

Abraham looked at her with kindness in his eyes.

"I am a man of means. It would be my privilege to pay for your passage."

"I could not accept that."

"I have more money than I need and more than a man of my circumstances could spend in a lifetime."

Ruby could not help but banter a bit.

"No man knows how much he can spend until he tries."

"Perhaps not. But since I have no intention of undertaking such an experiment, I am unlikely to be in need. I beg you to take this gift from me."

"You are an angel."

"I am not an angel. I am an erring and imperfect man. But there is a quality that all men have in common with the angels— the ability to bring happiness to others."

The day whispered of autumn when Ruby arrived at Boston Harbor for the journey home. Abraham accompanied her to the pier. He had paid for her to be a cabin passenger.

"I will miss our conversations and walks," Abraham told her as they readied to part. "But it is the expectation of one such as myself, and indeed of all men, that some of those we care about will have more meaningful attachments and leave us. If you love Edwin as you say you do, he must be a good man. And no good man could resist you. I take joy in knowing that the best part of your life lies ahead."

"I shall never forget your kindness," Ruby said. "You are a friend, as good as any in the world. If it had not mercifully come to pass that I had you to comfort me, I might have gone mad. For so long as my heart beats, I will treasure the remembrance of all that you have given to me."

Ruby dropped to one knee, held Abraham by the shoulders, and drew him close.

"This is the opposite of the way things are done in fairy tales," he said as he returned Ruby's embrace. "The prince is supposed to kneel down before the beautiful princess."

"Whatever your height, I would kneel down in thanks for all that you have done."

"You will write to me, I hope."

"I will; I promise. One day, perhaps, we shall see each other again."

Ruby boarded the ship and waved to Abraham as the vessel moved away from the pier. The distance between them was such that she could neither see the tears that streamed down his cheeks nor hear his sobs.

※

Marie, Octavius Joy, and I bade Edwin farewell at Euston Railway Station as he began the first leg of the journey that would take him to Liverpool and then to Boston. Edwin had read about Henry Hudson, Walter Raleigh, and other famous men who had travelled to America. This was a quest of a different order.

The sun was rising in the sky the following morning when Edwin boarded the ship in Liverpool. He carried Ruby's letter with him. There was no need of light to read it, for he knew its contents by heart. Ruby's address was written on a piece of paper and also fixed in his mind. He thought about what the moment would be like when they first saw each other again.

Had fate not intervened, he might, in a matter of days, have seen the outline of her ship on the horizon.

▼

Ruby had enough of good looks that men were almost always pleasant to her. Her kind manner encouraged similar treatment. The servant staff on the ship to England accorded her additional deference because of her status as a cabin passenger.

The food in cabin class was well prepared and served in a private dining room. An area of the deck was reserved for fresh air games. Backgammon, chess, and cards—all foreign to her—were played in the salon.

There are very few emigrants from America to England. The steerage area was filled mostly with cargo. She visited the few passengers lodged amidst the crates and brought them small favors from cabin service from time to time.

At night, Ruby stood on the ship's deck and gazed at the moon and stars. The stars rose in immeasurable space, infinite in their number. She thought often of the circumstances under which she had last travelled across the ocean. The stars had different meaning to her now.

She knew that Marie and I would be joyous to see her. Her confidence was growing with regard to Edwin.

What was meant to be would be. And she was going home.

Then there was a change in the weather.

It was late afternoon near sunset. The wind and the waves were restless. There was a murky confusion of flying clouds, tossed up into thick heaps. Seasoned seamen shook their heads and looked uneasily about.

"That's a remarkable sky," one of them said. "I don't remember one like it. There will be mischief tonight."

Brooding black clouds spread a sullen darkness until the sky was a heavy colour. The night grew darker. Lightning flashed and quivered. The ceiling of the world could not have been more dark if the sun, moon, and stars had fallen from the Heavens.

The wind grew more angry. Large drops of rain began to fall as if each drop were a leaden bead. The wind sent the rain slanting down at strange angles. For a moment, it would die away and Ruby could delude herself into believing that it had laid itself to rest. Then she heard the wind growling again, gathering strength as huge waves crashed against the ship.

The thunder rolled louder, as though through the halls of an ancient temple in the sky. The lightning became fiercer and more dazzling. Rain poured down like Heaven's wrath.

The ship moved forward gallantly against the elements, its tall masts trembling. Onward it surged, high now upon the curling billows, now low in the hollows of the sea as though hiding for a moment from the fury of the storm.

Nature raged against the ship's boldness. Angry waves rose up their hoary heads, dashing themselves against the vessel. The rolling of the ship became more severe. Had the ship ever taken a roll before like the one just passed? Worse still, like the one that is coming? Can it bear the mass of water that it is taking on board, beating at the closed windows and doors?

Gusting rain poured down like showers of steel. Undulating hills changed to valleys. Undulating valleys lifted up to hills. Masses of water shivered and shook with a booming sound.

Imagine a human face upon a vessel's prow with a thousand monstrous warriors bent upon driving it back, smashing it between the eyes whenever it attempts to advance an inch. Imagine the ship with every artery of its huge body swollen and bursting under this maltreatment, struggling to stay afloat or die. Imagine the wind howling, the sea roaring, the rain beating, all in furious array. Picture the sky, dark and wild, the clouds in fearful sympathy with the waves, the loud hoarse shouts of seamen, the rush of water through every opening, and the striking of the heavy sea upon the deck.

The ship was at the mercy of the storm, and the storm had no mercy. There was such whirl and tumult that nature itself seemed mad. The ship spun round and round, then down onto its side with its masts dipping into the waves. Springing up, it rolled over onto the other side until the sea struck again with the roar of a thousand cannons and hurled it upright.

The vessel staggered and shivered as though stunned. Every plank groaned. Every nail shrieked. It was as though an angry god had summoned up monsters beyond imagination from the deep in a violent effort to beat the ship down. The air was thick with phantoms, spirits, leaping, flying, raging, howling, thrashing with knotted whips and chains.

In one dreadful moment, the waves struck with violence enough to send a heavy wood beam through the side of the ship where Ruby's quarters lay. There was grinding and crashing and a rushing in of water. Ruby was flung against the cabin wall. The ship tilted. Another wave gushed in and out, taking Ruby with it.

She screamed in horror . . . Falling . . . Falling . . . Sucked into the ocean . . . More waves . . . She gasped desperately to breathe . . . There was another massive wave.

The ship somehow was still upright. But it was moving away.

A useless cry of terror escaped Ruby's lips. She struggled in mortal combat with the sea to keep her head above the dark raging water.

She fell beneath the waves. Now she was above them, beating at the water with her hands. Looking round with desperate eyes, she saw a long dark spar beside her. A piece of wood torn loose by the collision between the ship and the sea. She grasped on to the fragment and clung to it for life.

The sea has no appreciation of good and evil. It treats them both the same.

The rain diminished. The thunder died away. The storm gave way to calm.

Hours passed. Ruby did not know how many. She knew only that the struggle of her life was almost done. The wooden spar, soaked through with water, was beginning to sink, taking with it her last hope of survival.

She thought of Christopher and how bravely he had faced death. She thought of Marie and all the others she had loved.

Most of all, she thought of Edwin.

She would never look upon his face or hear his voice again.

There would be no plot of land in a churchyard, where those who loved her could mourn.

The water murmured an invitation to rest. There was a final splash and struggle. Ruby could fight no more. The voyage home that had begun with so much hope was ending.

The sea closed over Ruby's head. The ocean floor would be her grave.

❦

The storm had passed. The sun had come up. The sea was calm. Edwin stood on the deck of the ship that was carrying him to America.

The crew had been instructed to keep an eye out for lifeboats. Edwin was flanked by two seamen. They were looking over the water. Edwin thought he saw a body bobbing up and down.

One of the seamen said it was not so. The other was unsure and called for a pair of field glasses. Through the lenses, he saw a woman amidst the waves.

The ship's own lifeboats were useless. They had been crushed like walnut shells by the blows of the sea.

The two seamen volunteered to go down on ropes into the ocean.

"You risk your lives," the captain told them.

They were heroes, both.

Men ran with long thick ropes. A rope was tied round each seaman's waist, another round the upper portion of his chest. The seamen leaped into the ocean, trusting in those who held the twined fiber. Striving valiantly, they swam toward the drowning figure.

Under it went, then back to the surface.

The two seamen were close enough now to know that it was a woman. With a few more vigorous strokes, they would reach her.

The woman's final struggle agitated the rippling water. Slowly, she disappeared from view.

The spot where she went under was undistinguishable from all that had surrounded her.

One of the seamen dove beneath the surface and groped for her in the dark. Feeling her within his grasp, he clasped her tight. The men on board pulled hard on the ropes and hauled them in like fish.

The woman was laid out flat on the ship's hard wooden deck.

Edwin stared at the pale limp form, then fell to his knees in the recognition. His tears fell upon Ruby's face, mingling with water from the sea.

He kissed Ruby's cold wet lips.

"I beg of you, God. Spare her life. Grant me this wish, and I will hold you beside her in my heart for eternity."

A seaman felt for Ruby's pulse.

"There is life in her," he said.

Hope surged in Edwin's breast. He put his lips to Ruby's, trying desperately to breathe life into her.

She lay still.

He breathed more.

A thin stream of seawater trickled from Ruby's mouth . . . Her chest expanded.

"She is breathing," one of the seamen said.

Edwin smoothed the hair away from Ruby's forehead. His shadow fell upon her like the light of a loving sun.

Ruby felt the touch of a trembling hand, opened her eyes, and saw a face between her and the sky. The face of a man, young and handsome, shaded by rich dark hair. A face that she had dreamed of, waking and sleeping, from the day that she first saw it.

Edwin gazed lovingly down upon her.

"I have died and gone to Heaven," Ruby Spriggs said.

Book 4

CHAPTER 13

It did not take long for Ruby to come to her senses after being rescued from the sea. Most of us hope to enter Heaven someday. But she was pleased to find that she was still of this world and joyful beyond measure to be with Edwin.

Several days passed before their ship arrived in Boston. During that time, they shared every detail of what had happened to tear them apart and what had transpired during their separation.

"It was foolish of me to do what I did," Ruby acknowledged.

"Foolish, but very brave."

Edwin sat close by her side.

"Promise that you will never leave me again," he said.

"I would not lose you again for all the treasures of the world."

Edwin wrote a letter to Octavius Joy while they were on board ship, telling him that Ruby was safe following a harrowing storm and that they would return soon to England. Ruby wrote a similar letter to Marie. On the day that they arrived in Boston, they took both letters to the Collins Steamship Office for posting to London.

They went next to the Boston Book Emporium, where Abraham Hart greeted them with astonishment.

"I had feared that I would never see you again," he told Ruby. "This reunion is sooner than I could have hoped for. Indeed, it has come so swiftly that there has been little time for hoping."

Edwin told Abraham how pleased he was to meet him.

"You have done us many acts of kindness that can never be fully repaid."

"No payment is necessary," Abraham answered. "The reward one receives for kindness is that one enjoys being kind."

Later, Ruby and Edwin were alone. The bright sun was nearing the end of its day. The colours of twilight were no less beautiful but of a quieter tint than those that had come before.

They walked hand in hand. All seemed right with the world.

Edwin held Ruby's hand more tightly. Then he dropped to one knee.

"Dear Ruby, I have loved you from the moment I first saw you. No one could make me happier than you make me."

Her heart beat rapidly. She had hoped from the start that it would come to this.

"I would like very much for us to spend our lives together. Will you marry me?"

Tears of joy flowed from Ruby's eyes. And from her full young heart came her reply: "You know I will."

The church where they were married had a cracked stone floor and old oak roof. Leaves of ivy tapped gently at the windows, leaving the pews in tempting shade.

The hand of Providence was in their union. There could have been no clearer signal from the Almighty Creator that He had bestowed his blessing upon them than the manner in which Ruby was saved from the sea.

The sun was shining through the stained glass window of the church when they said their wedding vows. The bride was given away by Abraham Hart. When Ruby and Edwin stood before the altar and the preacher asked, "Who giveth this woman to be married to this man?" Abraham answered in the same clear voice that Ruby had first heard at Lucretia Mott's town meeting.

Then came the vows.

"This day, I take the happiest and best step of my life . . . I will cherish you with a love and trust that do not die . . . I would not forsake your hand in marriage for any other blessing that life can offer . . . We may grow rich. God willing, we will grow old. But rich or poor, old or young, we shall be the same to each other."

None of us has a full understanding of where we are in the whirling wheel of life until some marked stop brings a clear perception to us. This was such a day. Ruby had left everything she loved and crossed the ocean into the unknown, believing that it would help Edwin. Now she would be returning home as Edwin's wife and with greater joy than if he were the stateliest lord in England.

When the ceremony was over, Ruby could not conceal her joy.

"I am Edwin's bride," she all but shouted.

Abraham swore that the old church bells rang more cheerfully that day than ever before.

After her previous experience at sea, Ruby would have preferred to return to England by horse-drawn carriage. But the path home lay through the ocean, so she consented to board a ship again.

It was a splendid New England autumn with brightly coloured leaves on the day that she and Edwin left Boston. Abraham accompanied them to the pier.

"I hope that this is not the last time we meet," Edwin said in parting. "But if it is, please know that you will always have our gratitude and affection."

"I am extremely fond of your wife," Abraham responded. "It comforts me to know that she will be with someone who loves her as she deserves. Your happiness will be mine."

Then Abraham turned to Ruby.

"Though you be far away, I shall think of you every day. When I look upon Edwin, for as short a time as I have known him, I know in my heart that, were the decision mine, I would have chosen him to be your husband."

Ruby had never shown as much interest in the state of the weather as she did on board the ship to England. But the voyage was marked by calm seas and a gentle favouring wind. With Edwin beside her, she felt as though she were guarded by the entire British navy.

There was a grandeur in the stately ship's motion as it slashed nobly through the sea. A bright sun lit its course by day. The reflection of the moon on the water at night seemed a map to home.

Then came a crisp fair morning. Ruby and Edwin would never forget the day. There was a cloudless sky and bracing air. The water danced and sparkled round the great ship's hull, full of motion and free. Before them lay the most glorious of sights. A speck of land glittering in the sun. Home. The shores of England.

There was a train ride to London.

A joyous reunion.

I am not ashamed to say that I wept to see them.

Soon after, Octavius Joy hosted a wedding party in their honour. The cake glistened with frosted sugar and was garnished with a little Cupid under a barley-sugar arch. Mr. Joy made a toast in which he told of knowing Ruby since the age of three. He then chided her lovingly for her flight from London, while conceding, "One does not always find an old head upon young shoulders."

Ruby looked more of a woman than when she had gone away. The joy in her eyes made her face more lovely than ever.

"I have never seen you as beautiful as you are now," I told her.

"I have never been so happy."

At the end of the party, Marie and Ruby embraced.

"I left you once," Ruby told her. "Now I leave you again for another home."

"But this time, I am happy," Marie said. "With your marriage to Edwin, my own future is brighter than it was before. Someday, when your hair is grey, you will understand."

Then Marie embraced Edwin.

"For many years, I have had a kind and loving daughter. Now I also have a son."

When the first emotions of their new life had passed, Ruby and Edwin understood even more fully how fortunate they were. The richest men in England would have been proud to call Ruby their wife, and would have praised fate had a man such as Edwin married their daughter.

Edwin began work with Octavius Joy as the administrator of his charitable ventures. Mr. Joy placed great confidence in him, and Edwin was faithful to his trust. He brought all of the energy and determination that were natural to his character to the task.

With Edwin's help, a second learning center opened in London. Like the first, it encouraged women, as well as men, to learn to read and write.

Octavius Joy also embarked upon a plan to train teachers.

"It is necessary," he said. "Any man who has proven his unfitness for any other occupation is free, without examination or qualification, to open a school. That must change."

Edwin marveled often on how fate had moved him from being a protégé of Alexander Murd to a protégé of Octavius Joy.

As for Murd's fate, reality took a wolfish turn.

Octavius Joy had spoken with men of influence in the government. He was on good terms with them and played the game well.

Government officials, elected and appointed, respond to the public will when forced to do so. The undeniable fact that women and children had died while working illegally underground in the Lancashire mine led to expressions of public outrage that weighed more heavily than Murd's influence. Justice was soon tracking him with a strong scent and steady tread.

The prison gates are heavy, and the keys that turn them are strong. Men who had conspired illegally with Murd found the thought of such a key turning against them to be exceedingly unpleasant. One by one, they unburdened themselves to the authorities in the hope of lenient treatment.

Harold Plepman, who had come to Murd's office seeking a greater bribe, confessed to his wrongdoing. That opened the door to more confessions by purchasing agents.

A committee was established by Parliament to investigate the Lancashire mine disaster. That led the authorities to coroner Samuel Shaw, who also turned on Murd.

Murd himself was called to testify before the Parliamentary committee. Then he was summoned to a new coroner's inquest in Lancashire.

It was December and very cold when Murd arrived in the mining town. Snow had fallen, but was grey with soot before it touched the ground.

Murd intended to establish himself at the inquest as a man of substance. He was attired in a fine suit with leather boots, polished. The boots cost more than a miner would earn for a full month's work.

The inquest room was crowded with miners.

"You have no heart," one of them shouted out when Murd entered.

"The facts established by Doctor William Harvey make it clear that I have a heart," Murd arrogantly responded. "The circulation of the blood cannot be carried on without one."

"We do not have the same fancy airs and book learning as you. But you will hear what we have to say."

"I will not flatter you with my attention. Nothing could be further from my thoughts."

"You call yourself a gentleman, but you are nothing of the kind."

"I am a man of business, not a priest."

Murd was not sorry for anything that he had done. The operation of his mines was satisfactorily settled in his mind. He was sorry only because consequences of a troubling kind were now likely at hand.

The solicitor for the Parliamentary committee aggressively questioned Murd. So did the coroner.

"You seem to be prejudged against me," Murd told the coroner.

"I have not stated an opinion. I have asked a question. I will base my opinion on what you tell me."

In the third hour of testimony, an issue arose as to whether adequate timber was currently in place to support the sides of the Lancashire mine shaft.

"We can resolve the issue by visiting the mine," the government solicitor suggested.

Murd did not like the idea.

"We will do it," the coroner ruled.

Murd knew of the miners' existence through his business. He knew how much coal a given number of them could bring to the surface in a given period of time. He knew them as crowds of ants, burrowing and toiling underground. But he knew more about the ways of insects from his science studies in school than he knew of the miners as individuals.

Now, as Murd walked to the pit with his eyes fixed upon the ground, he was surrounded by them.

They reached the shaft, and a voice cried out, "Let him go into the mine."

There were cries of assent.

Murd was feeling danger now. The coroner and government solicitor were standing back. His own solicitor was not in sight. The mob was in control.

Murd laid a hand on one of the miner's shoulders and sought to appease the crowd.

"My dear friends. You are blinded with passion. It is natural, very natural. But you do not know friend from foe."

"We know the difference well," a miner shouted. "Into the mine you go."

"You are being hasty," Murd pled.

"Are you a coward?"

The crowd surged threateningly forward. Murd moved closer to the top of the shaft to avoid being touched.

"You do not have the courage to go into your own mine," a miner taunted.

"No man will go down the shaft again until you see with your own eyes what it is like," another shouted.

The countenances of men who have undergone a particularly cruel captivity bear a record of their ordeal that never fades away. Murd now saw that look on the faces around him.

"Your gold is red with our blood."

Murd looked down into the shaft. One of the miners took a stone and threw it into the pit. The stone could not be heard when it landed.

"It is a deep one," the miner said.

The mob was crowding closer now. Murd thought desperately of running away and tearing through the streets. But no path was open for escape. And humiliation before these savages was unacceptable.

Murd stepped into the bucket that carried men to the bottom of the shaft. The composure drained from his face. He was trapped, caged like an animal.

Three miners joined him.

"Lower him down the shaft," someone in the crowd shouted.

There was a raucous cheer of approval.

The descent began. Murd's face was white, as though covered with ash. He was sweating profusely despite the frigid cold.

The bucket descended into darkness. Murd imagined that the walls of the shaft were closing in to crush him. His breath was laboured.

The bucket hit bottom.

"I have seen enough," Murd said. "Let us go back to the surface."

"No, governour. Now we go into the tunnels."

A groan escaped Murd's lips, as though he had been wounded by a cruel weapon. A look of terror came into his eyes. The men prodded him forward.

They crawled into a tunnel on hands and knees with two lamps to guide them. The tunnel was no longer a source of coal. The miners had followed it one hundred yards to the end of a vein long ago. Two other tunnels extended off of it. One of those had also been fully mined.

Horror fell upon Murd like a spectral hand, not as a thought but as a bodily sensation. A long dark winding way lay between him and the place far above ground where men lived. The entangling forest of dead wood—the crosspieces, bars, and beams that supported the tunnel—was frighteningly fragile. A low deep voice seemed to cry out from the ground: "What visitor is this in Hades?"

One word felt traced by an eternal finger in the drops of cold sweat upon his brow—Death.

There are rats in the tunnels, some of them as big as cats. The miners leave them alone, and the rats pass the miners by. They want no more to do with the miners than the miners want to do with them.

Crawling forward, Murd came face to face with a rat.

He swiped at it. The rat bit him on the hand.

And Murd lost what was left of his reason. His scream sounded like death upon the wing. He managed somehow to turn himself around, grabbed one of the miners' lamps, and slithered like a terrified snake back through the tunnel toward the shaft.

The tunnels are a maze. Murd took a wrong turn. The top of his lamp fell off.

Then the miners heard an explosion. The earth shook. A rush of wind and dust blew past them.

When the dust subsided, the miners searched for Murd as though he were one of their own. They found him. He was alive. They brought him to the surface. Parts of his body were burned black. In other places, the skin had peeled off as though he had been dropped in boiling water.

He did not live long. There was a rattling noise in his throat, a short stifled moan. And Alexander Murd lay dead.

It was hard to believe that he had once been a child who said his prayers at his mother's knee before lying down in bed at night and falling into an innocent slumber.

After Murd's passing, the proper authorities were brought in and took possession of his remains. There was a coroner's inquest. The ruling of the coroner's jury was "Accidental Death."

Edwin had sad feelings about the matter. Recalling his own brief experience in the mine shaft, he understood the terror that Murd had felt and the horrible nature of his end. After much thought—and with Ruby's approval—he sent a letter of condolence to Isabella, but never received a response.

Ruby's time of hardship soon receded into memory like a nightmare that vanishes with the morning sun. When she thought of her lonely ocean voyage to America, she always thought next of the kindness that Abraham Hart had shown to her, and it made her happier than if she had not journeyed across the sea.

She wrote often to Abraham. At the end of each letter, Edwin added words of friendship in his own hand.

There was much to tell.

It was not long before a little boy named Christopher Octavius Chatfield was seen crawling about their home. His room was decorated with a rainbow of colours, since Ruby was quite certain that babies notice colours from birth.

As Christopher learned to walk, there was a little girl with the face of her mother, whom they named Marie Rebecca. And then another little boy.

Three children, born of tenderness and passion joined.

It gave Abraham great joy when he received a letter informing him that Anthony Abraham Chatfield had been born. Soon after, he wrote to Ruby and Edwin, telling them that he had taken a bride named Margaret and would like to bring her to England to meet his dear friends.

"To satisfy your polite curiosity," Abraham noted in a postscript, "Margaret is short in stature, but proportioned like those in the general population."

There was a joyful reunion in London. Ruby and Edwin found Margaret to be delightful. Abraham also met Octavius Joy, who insisted that he and Margaret abandon their hotel immediately and spend the rest of their time in London as guests in his home.

Mr. Joy and Abraham got along as well as two men can and spent considerable time in Mr. Joy's library, which Abraham pronounced a finer collection than that found within the walls of his own bookshop.

Abraham and Margaret also spent considerable time in Edwin and Ruby's home, listening happily to the tread of tiny feet, the sound of prattling words, and children laughing.

At the end of their visit, Edwin told them, "You will always have family and a home where you are welcome in England."

Meanwhile, as Edwin and Ruby were building their life together, Octavius Joy, like the rest of us, was growing older.

Father Time tarries for no man. But he lays his hand lightly at times upon those who have used him well. Mr. Joy grew old inexorably enough, but remained hale and hearty with a young spirit. His grey head was but a sign that God had given him His blessing.

"I am in want of nothing," Octavius Joy said from time to time. "When my strength fails me, if I can take my leave quick and quiet, I shall be content."

He continued to mentor Edwin, speaking often to the younger man about the pleasure and fulfillment of living a principled life.

"Man enjoys the most exalted position in life's creative plan," Mr. Joy would counsel. "We must always strive to justify that privilege. No one flies to Heaven on wings of words. Conduct is the key. The life of every person we can help is precious. Every man, woman, and child matters."

As Octavius Joy aged further, his face remained contented with a smile in every wrinkle. There was a calm sunset air about him. He was at peace with himself and the world.

There is a time for all things. Sadly, in Octavius Joy's eightieth year, there came a time for him to die.

His affairs were in perfect order and so systematically wound up that it was as though he had dictated the terms of his end.

On the final day of Mr. Joy's life, he visited a learning center. Upon returning home, he told his housekeeper that he felt a slight uneasiness of breath. He went to his library to read. When he did not appear for dinner at the usual hour, the housekeeper knocked gently on the door. There was no answer, so she opened the door and saw him seated in his most comfortable chair with a book in hand. He seemed to be absorbed in meditation, which at first she hoped he was. A bell-rope hung within his reach, but he had not moved toward it. He was dead.

Death is a natural part of life. It is as certain as being born, although its arrival cannot be calculated with the same precision. Octavius Joy's death, like his life, was gentle and kind. On the day after his passing, his solicitor gave a letter to Edwin and Ruby that Mr. Joy had written for them:

My Dearest Edwin and Ruby,

I am very sorry to leave you. But I am called, and I must go. Do not grieve for me. I have lived a wonderful life.

If God had given me children of my own blood, I would have wished for them to be just like you. May your lives be as long and happy as mine has been.

My love will always be with you,
Octavius

In due course, Mr. Joy's estate was settled. His Last Will and Testament bequeathed separately to Marie and myself one hundred pounds annually for the duration of our lives. There were bequests to others, including annuities to his housekeeper and others who had maintained his home.

The house and everything in it, including Mr. Joy's books, were bequeathed to Edwin and Ruby. "It gives me great pleasure," his Last Will and Testament read, "to know that the home that I have been so happy in for so many years will remain a joyous place."

The remainder of Mr. Joy's estate amounted to several hundred thousand pounds. This was put into a trust to fund learning centers, those already in existence and also those that might be established in the future.

Edwin was named in Mr. Joy's Last Will and Testament as the Administrator of the trust with a generous annual salary.

"The ability to read becomes part of one's character," Mr. Joy stated in the closing paragraph of his Will. "A life without the ability to read is like entering a cathedral and looking at the stained glass windows at night."

There are often wide distinctions between knowledge, wealth, and greatness. Some men know each planet by its Latin name as a consequence of their studies in school. But they know nothing of charity, mercy, and love.

Octavius Joy was cut from different cloth. He was a man of the highest principles, pointing ever upward. He set himself against ignorance and poverty, and made that battle his life's work. He was ready at all times to give something of his own to help someone else. He advocated education for all, but understood that a loving heart is a necessary complement to knowledge. To the extent that he sought power, it was the power to do good.

The chief pleasure of Mr. Joy's life was giving to others the means to achieve a better life for themselves. He spoke his mind without duplicity. His courtesy never failed him. The desire to do good animated his being until the last moment of his existence on this planet.

There is a cold stone marker in the cemetery where Octavius Joy is buried that states the dates of his birth and death. But his true monument is the thousands of English men and women and their children who can read and write today and have better lives as a consequence of his generosity and kindness.

I am certain that the Lord smiled upon him at the end of his days and said of his life, "Well done."

Shortly after Octavius Joy's death, Edwin found a portrait of Mr. Joy in the attic. He and Ruby hung it in the dining room after they moved into their new home. Thus, Mr. Joy is a companion to them at dinner every night.

In the years that followed, Edwin more than justified his mentor's good opinion of him. It is in his nature to lead, and people feel comfortable following him.

Like Mr. Joy, Edwin has been steadfast in his determination that opportunity be given to others. He works tirelessly to better the lives of the downtrodden by opening doors to the knowledge that comes with learning to read and write.

One of the learning centers that Edwin has established is in Lancashire.

And now there is one more happening that I must tell.

Mature love is quiet in expressing itself. Its voice is low. It is modest and retiring.

On the day that Ruby and Edwin returned to England, Marie and I were joyful.

"It is a wonderful thing," Marie said to me that evening, "to see young people that we are so fond of brought together with a lifetime of happiness before them."

"It is almost enough to make the two of us get married," said I.

"Nonsense," Marie responded with a laugh. "We are too old for that."

"We are too old to be single. Why should we not be married instead of sitting through long evenings by our solitary firesides? Let us marry and make one fireside of it."

"You are joking."

"I am not."

"You are making fun of me."

She was blushing now.

"I will marry you, Marie, if you will consent to marry me."

"People would laugh at us."

"Let them laugh. We have laughed heartily together for many years."

A twinkle and a tear glistened in her eye.

"Will you marry me, my dear?"

"Yes," Marie answered. "I would very much like to marry you."

We have one bakery now and one home. We are not as young as we once were, but we are as light of heart as ever. Marie sits often at night with needle and wool by the fire. I watch as she knits and see a face that is happy and serene.

And now my story is done. Like life, it includes grief and trial and sorrow. Had I only happiness to tell of, this reading would have been very short.

There are dark shadows on the earth. I know that. But darkness means that the light we see is stronger in the contrast. Setting all of the world's good against its evil, I believe that we live on a most respectable planet.

Love is the thing that matters most. It is stronger than all the evil in the world. I think often of those I have known and loved and who are now gone. They touch the chords of my memory softly and harmoniously.

Ruby and Edwin have also lost some who are dear to them. Hearts that they once loved have ceased to beat. Hands that they grasped have grown cold. Eyes that they sought out lie hidden in the grave. But it is the fate of all who mingle with the world and attain the prime of life to lose some of those we love.

It is best to have a loving heart, even if at times it is bruised and broken.

Ruby and Edwin are one in heart, one in mind, and one in soul. They are equal in everything that they do within their home. Meeting them for the first time, one might suppose that they are lovers only recently wed, such is the tenderness between them. Edwin's eyes brighten whenever Ruby's name is mentioned. She smiles when she hears his name. Each year that passes seems the happiest of their lives.

Even in the darkest nights of winter, their house is bright and merry. They read aloud to the children, the oldest of whom now reads aloud to his younger brother and sister.

Sometimes in the evening after they have put the children to bed, Ruby sits quietly and simply looks at Edwin. He is even more dear to her now than when she crossed the sea on her lonely voyage to America. Edwin never lies down in bed at night without giving thanks that she is beside him. Through all of life's emotions, they are each other's most steadfast friend. What a treasure they have in one another.

For so many years, Ruby has filled my heart with happiness. I remember her as she was on the first day that she and Christopher stood outside my bakery. A tiny, hungry, ill-clothed child, shivering in the cold. I remember her as she grew older, learning to read and write, talking and laughing in Marie's home, in love with all about her.

Ruby and Edwin bring their children to the bakery to visit often. They are always welcome. Each time they come, I give the children bread with strawberry jam.

Printed in the United States
by Baker & Taylor Publisher Services